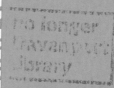

FELL DOWN

BOOKS BY M. E. KERR

Dinky Hocker Shoots Smack!
Best of the Best Books (YA) 1970–83 (ALA)
Best Children's Books of 1972, *School Library Journal*
ALA Notable Children's Books of 1972

If I Love You, Am I Trapped Forever?
Honor Book, *Book World* Children's Spring Book Festival,
1973
Outstanding Children's Books of 1973, *The New York Times*

The Son of Someone Famous
(AN URSULA NORDSTROM BOOK)
Best Children's Books of 1974, *School Library Journal*
"Best of the Best" Children's Books 1966–1978, *School
Library Journal*

Is That You, Miss Blue?
(AN URSULA NORDSTROM BOOK)
Outstanding Children's Books of 1975, *The New York Times*
ALA Notable Children's Books of 1975
Best Books for Young Adults, 1975 (ALA)

Love Is a Missing Person
(AN URSULA NORDSTROM BOOK)

I'll Love You When You're More Like Me
(AN URSULA NORDSTROM BOOK)
Best Children's Books of 1977, *School Library Journal*

Gentlehands
(AN URSULA NORDSTROM BOOK)
Best Books for Young Adults, 1978 (ALA)
ALA Notable Children's Books of 1978
Best Children's Books of 1978, *School Library Journal*
Winner, 1978 Christopher Award
Best Children's Books of 1978, *The New York Times*

Little Little
ALA Notable Children's Books of 1981
Best Books for Young Adults, 1981 (ALA)
Best Children's Books of 1981, *School Library Journal*
Winner, 1981 Golden Kite Award, Society of Children's
Book Writers

What I Really Think of You
(A CHARLOTTE ZOLOTOW BOOK)
Best Children's Books of 1982, *School Library Journal*

Me Me Me Me Me: Not a Novel
(A CHARLOTTE ZOLOTOW BOOK)
Best Books for Young Adults, 1983 (ALA)

Him *She Loves?*
(A CHARLOTTE ZOLOTOW BOOK)

I Stay Near You
(A CHARLOTTE ZOLOTOW BOOK)
Best Books for Young Adults, 1985 (ALA)

Night Kites
(A CHARLOTTE ZOLOTOW BOOK)
Best Books for Young Adults, 1986 (ALA)
Recommended Books for Reluctant YA Readers, 1987
(ALA)

Fell
(A CHARLOTTE ZOLOTOW BOOK)
Best Books for Young Adults, 1987 (ALA)

Fell Back
(A CHARLOTTE ZOLOTOW BOOK)
Finalist, 1990 Edgar Allan Poe Award, Best Young Adult
Mystery (Mystery Writers of America)

M.E. KERR
FELL DOWN

A Charlotte Zolotow Book
An Imprint of HarperCollins*Publishers*

Fell Down
Copyright © 1991 by M. E. Kerr
1 2 3 4 5 6 7 8 9 10
First Edition

Library of Congress Cataloging-in-Publication Data
Kerr, M. E.
Fell down / by M.E. Kerr.
p.   cm.
"A Charlotte Zolotow book."
Summary : Seventeen-year-old Fell's determination to investigate
his best friend's death in a car crash leads him to a ventriloquists
convention and an unsolved disappearance from almost twenty years ago.
ISBN 0-06-021763-4. — ISBN 0-06-021764-2 (lib. bdg.)
[1. Ventriloquism—Fiction. 2. Mystery and detective stories .]
I. Title .
PZ7.K46825F i 1991   90-49921
[Fic}—dc20   CIP
                                                                    AC

Tom Baird was my oldest and dearest friend and this book is to remember him.

So long, dear Tom.

Little Jack Horner

Sat in the corner,

Eating a Christmas pie;

He put in his thumb,

And pulled out a plum . . .

—Old nursery rhyme

THE MOUTH

These be

Three silent things:

The falling snow . . . the hour

Before the dawn . . . the mouth of one

Just dead.

—Adelaide Crapsey

FELL DOWN

1

"Fell, you're a mess," Keats said, "and you're wallowing in it."

"I don't want to talk about it now."

"Then when?"

The waiter asked if he could tell us the specials.

It wouldn't have surprised me if Keats had made him stand there while I explained all the deep trouble my mind was in, but instead she listened to him. Then she said she'd have the fettuccine with seafood.

I ordered the Long Island duck.

"You look awful, too," Keats said while the waiter was taking the menus from our hands.

"Thanks for pointing that out," I said.

"I should have suggested someplace tacky for dinner. Not here," she continued.

We were in the Edwardian Room, in the Plaza Hotel. She'd come all the way into New York City to take me out. I knew that it was really Daddy who would pay the charge: Lawrence O. Keating, an architect whose dreams for his only daughter did not include John Fell.

He didn't have to worry about it anymore. We were just friends, though he'd never believe it.

"Promise me one thing before you tell me what this is all about," she said.

"Okay. One thing."

"When your food comes, don't tell me what's wrong with it. Don't taste mine and tell me what's wrong with mine. If something's overpowered by its sauce or underseasoned, keep it a secret, okay? I like to think everything's wonderful."

"At these prices, I don't blame you."

"Even if we were eating at McDonald's, I'd feel the same way, Fell. Who wants to hear a whole critique? Just eat, drink, and be merry."

"Give me a break," I said. "I don't complain that much."

"Yes you do. If you don't, you've changed."

"Well, yeah. That I've done."

"Talk!" she said.

"What do you want to know?"

"Why you're a jet crash."

"I wrote you about it."

"You said a close friend died in an automobile accident. But since when do you go to pieces over a friend's death? You didn't crack up when your dad died."

"No, I didn't."

"Maybe if you started back at the beginning," said Keats.

So I did. I told her Dib was my first friend at Gardner School, and maybe my only real friend there. I told her how we grew apart when I got into Sevens, the elite club on The Hill, with its own residence and clubhouse.

I told her how Dib took up with Jack Horner, known as Little Jack. I took the story up to the last time I saw Dib. He was getting into Little Jack's green Mustang. Little Jack had been drinking. Little Jack was driving.

My voice always played tricks on me at this point in the story, and I'd feel breathless, and a sting behind my eyes.

Keats said, "So you just left school—walked out and the heck with your final exams and everything."

"Yeah. I just walked out and the heck with my final exams and everything."

"So now you don't even have a high school diploma."

"*Nada*," I agreed.

"Fell, it's not like you. You stayed together when your father died."

"Don't keep saying that. . . .Maybe that's *why* I let go this time."

"Oh?"

She looked across at me. She smelled of Obsession and she had on something silky and green, to match her eyes. I was glad I was in this phony place with her, because I needed things to be familiar. I needed to believe the world hadn't changed.

She looked like she belonged in that roomy arm-chair she was sitting in, under the colossal chandelier.

I was out of place. I had on some old seersucker suit of my dad's that'd looked great in the 70's, and my bow tie was a clip-on. I didn't have the clothes or the energy to try and look like someone who belonged with the beautiful people. Keats didn't need any extra push to look that way. She was part of that scene. When we went someplace like that, the maitre d' always addressed all his remarks to her.

Keats thought a few seconds about what I'd said.

She said, "Are you saying that you're having a delayed reaction to your father's death?"

"I don't know what I'm having," I said.

"I think you're experiencing a displacement," Keats said. "That means you might let something big go by, and then later on, without knowing it, react the way you should have earlier over something much less important."

"My shrink would love you," I said.

"Fell! You're seeing a shrink? I can't believe this!"

"I was seeing one for a while. Mom insisted I at least talk to one. I didn't go more than three times. . . . Do you know what they cost?"

"Of course I know! I'm a graduate! I went for five years!"

"I remember."

6/FELL DOWN

"You must be hurting, Fell."

"Not anymore. Not *hurting*."

"What then?"

"I'm mad as hell, Keats. That's all."

"At yourself?"

"No, I'm over the self-blame, finally. I'm not over the feeling I'd like to get my hands on Little Jack."

"What would that solve, Fell?"

"It wouldn't solve anything. It'd satisfy something."

"Diogenes said forgiveness is better than revenge."

"You just made that up."

"No, he said it. I did a paper on him."

"I've never believed what *The Cottersville Compass* wrote about that accident. They claimed it was the guy who hit Dib and Little Jack who was drunk. . . . I *saw* Little Jack get behind the wheel drunk."

"Maybe they were both drunk. Who was the other guy?"

"Some stand-up comedian from Las Vegas."

The sommelier was circling. I always thought I looked twenty-one and not seventeen, but he wasn't fooled and passed on by with the wine list.

While we ate, I told Keats what little I knew about this man named Lenny Last. I only had one write-up in *The Compass* to go by. I'd read that on the train when I was leaving Gardner. Last had driven his old white Cadillac through a red light just as Little Jack turned the corner. Dib and Last were both killed.

Keats thought she might have heard the name . . . maybe from *The Tonight Show.* . . . I didn't push it. I wanted Keats to talk about herself, too. Mom had pointed out that I was so wrapped up in myself lately, I didn't show any interest in other people. I hadn't even realized Mom was dating the guy across the hall.

"Mom," I'd said, "you're *dating* that tailor?"

"What did you think I was doing with him?"

"Going to the movies with him, I don't know."

"That's *dating*, Johnny."

Keats told me she was going to become a psycho-analyst. Maybe not a psychoanalyst, she said, maybe just a therapist because she didn't think she could go through medical school.

"It's too hard," she said, "and it takes too long. . . . How's your duck?"

"It's good," I said. I didn't say that there wasn't enough sour cherry sauce on it, remembering my promise.

Keats said anything from Long Island had to be good.

She was most partial to her hometown, Seaville, in The Hamptons.

For a short time it'd been my hometown, too. Brooklyn would always be my real home, but some-times I remembered the ocean and the beaches, the roads winding through potato fields down to ponds with swans nesting there. The clean air and the blue sky and the smell of summer.

Keats glanced across the table at me and said sud-denly, "Let me drive you back there."

The restaurant where I worked was open seven

days, so we took turns getting weekends off. It wasn't my turn. But I wouldn't have minded heading out to The Hamptons, where so far there weren't people without homes sleeping in doorways and drug addicts stalking you. . . . All of that was hard enough to take when you were in good shape, but if you were on shaky ground, you had to wonder how long before *you'd* be out there, with everything you owned in a shopping cart you'd stolen from a supermarket.

"What would Daddy say if you showed up with me?" I asked her.

"I didn't mean Seaville, Fell. I meant let me drive you back to Gardner School. I've never seen the place."

"I could get my clothes, finally."

"And you could look up Little Jack. . . . He's a townie, right? So he'd be there."

"I'm sure he would."

"I think you need to tell him off."

"I need to wipe up a dirty floor with him, more."

"Whatever. . . . You haven't been back at all, have you?"

I shook my head. "If I want to graduate, I have to go back this fall."

"I thought Sevens was so powerful you could get away with anything."

"Sevens can't do anything about academics. I didn't take my finals." I shrugged. I wished I'd taken them. I must have been getting better, because I couldn't imagine myself just walking out on everything.

"I'd love to see Sevens House," she said.

"You're just being nice, Keats. Thanks, but you don't need to change your whole personality just because I'm having a nervous breakdown."

We both laughed. I figured that she couldn't care less about seeing some prep-school clubhouse now that she was a college girl. In the fall she'd be a sophomore at Sweetbriar, in Virginia.

Then she smiled at me. I'd always loved her smile. It made her look more sophisticated than she was, and gentler than she was, too, though I couldn't fault her in that regard this night.

"I need to get out of The Hamptons," she said. "August is two weeks away, and you know what August is like. What we never dreamed would ever find their way out to the South Fork arrives in August, along with all the shrinks who take the month off, and all their nut cases."

"You should definitely be a psychoanalyst," I said. "You have all the sensitivity one needs for that profession."

"Only if you'll be my first patient and listen to me."

"I thought you were supposed to listen to me."

"Fell, be serious for a minute. Do you think you'll repeat the year so you can get your diploma? You should. It's a very fancy school."

"I might get a job as a cook's apprentice and forget my high school diploma. All I want is to own a restaurant someday."

Keats nodded. "I know that. But it'd only be one more year out of your life."

I was working at a French place on the waterfront,

over in Brooklyn Heights. It was called Le Rêve. The Dream.

One night my boss had told me if I stuck with him, I could end up owning the place. He didn't have a child to pass it on to.

But you can't step into someone else's dream.

I can't, anyway.

"You know what's wrong with me, Fell?" said Keats, who had just set an all-time record for Keats, by going for over an hour without mentioning what was wrong with her.

"What's wrong with you?"

"I'm not in love. . . . Do you know how pointless everything is when you're not in love?"

I nodded. I knew.

"I don't even know why I'm shopping anymore."

"You still want to look great, and you do."

"Why do I want to look great?" she said. "Who for?"

"For whom," I said.

"Exactly! But I'm not sure you're sympathetic. Sometimes I think you hang on to that old romance with Delia so you don't have to deal with reality."

"I'm over Delia," I said. Do you know what an oxymoron is? It's the official name for something combining contradictory expressions. If that sounds complicated, just think of cold fire, or hot snow, or over Delia.

But I would never admit to anyone that she was still there. I'd rather agree to the idea that Little Jack didn't kill Dib, Lenny Last did.

"Keats," I said, "you're right. We need to get away."

1

THE MOUTH

Of course Lenny Last was not his real name.

In 1961, he was enrolled in Gardner School as Leonard Tralastski.

Until he'd won the scholarship to The Hill, his life had not amounted to a hill of beans.

I yawn and snore to think of it!

Get out the violins until we're past the part where little Lenny's daddy goes down flying a torpedo bomber in World War II.

On the very day the Japs surrendered, September 1, 1945, Baby Leonard was born.

Happy Birthday, Tralastski!

Just when the Japs were crying in their saki as their emperor surrendered in Tokyo Bay, Mommy's little sweetums was at Lenox Hill Hospital bawling in his crib.

I know, I know: We don't say Japs anymore. But when we did, back when we did, there was no sign that Leonard Tralastski would have anything but a very ordinary fate.

His long-suffering mother raised him in a tiny two-room apartment on the West Side in New York City.

He was never poor.

His long-suffering mother worked in Hosiery at Macy's six days a week, and several nights sold tickets at a nearby Loew's.

But in a way our boy was a poor thing: poor in spirit and in poor health. He was, for an eternity, this too-tall, too-skinny kid who suffered from severe asthma, from mild acne, and from growing up without a dad.

He had no friends, no knack for making any.

He spent most of his time talking to his own hand.

He had a white glove that he pulled over his right hand, then closed the hand to a fist. On the back of the glove he painted a face, a lipstick mouth where the thumb and forefinger met. The thing's mouth moved when Lenny moved his thumb.

He called it Handy.

Sometimes he'd entertain his mother with Handy.

LENNY: Good morning, Handy.

HANDY: What's good about it?

LENNY: Well, the sun's out.

HANDY: Whose son?

LENNY: *S-u-n!* Not s-o-n. The *s-u-n* is out.

HANDY: Who let it out?

FELL DOWN/13

Only a mother would have clapped after, and cheered an encore out of him.

She was his only cheerleader, until the day he got off the train in Trenton, New Jersey, and got on the Gardner School bus, bound for Cottersville, Pennsylvania.

He was going to prep school.

He was going to be a junior.

They say in this life you have a very narrow chance of meeting the one person who is your other: your double, your *doppelgänger*. It is not a romantic meeting but a meeting of the minds. Some say the souls. And it is agreed that had you two never found each other, as most do not, then neither one would rise to the heights or sink to the depths such a coupling often inspires or propels.

Folie à deux.

That's the official name for it.

Would Gilbert have written without Sullivan? Would Lewis have discovered anything without Clark? . . . Would Loeb have murdered without Leopold?

On that bus, on that autumn day in Bucks County, when the leaves were being torn from the trees by a bitter wind in an early snap, Lenny Tralastski met *his* other.

"Is this seat taken?" said he.

I am not going to introduce myself.

I will tell you the story of Lenny Last with as few asides as possible.

You'll notice that I take some liberties, the privilege

of any storyteller. . . . Maybe the dialogue isn't verba-
tim; maybe this one wasn't smiling, that one wasn't
frowning when I said he was.

It'll all come out in the wash.

Aside:
Folie à deux means simultaneous insanity.
It takes two to tango . . . to tangle, too.

2

"Keats, this is Mrs. Violet, the Sevens' housemother."

"Keats?" she said, raising one eyebrow the way she did when we'd do something she wasn't sure we should do.

"Helen Keating," Keats said.

"Keats. That's a nice nickname. I like that."

I thought of the fact I didn't even know Mrs. Violet's first name. I'd never seen her out of Sevens House, and I'd never imagined her having any other life.

"I didn't think you'd be here," I said. "Don't you ever take a vacation?"

She was all in white. When wasn't she? These thin-legged silk pants that grabbed her ankles, high heels, pearls under a flimsy blouse, and the blond hair loose, not held back in the bun as usual.

"I always go somewhere in summer," she said, "but now I have to help prepare for the girls."

"What girls?"

"The *girls*, Fell," she said. "The girls! Surely you know about it, or were you gone by the time it was announced?"

"We didn't go coed, I trust." I laughed a bit smugly.

"As a matter of fact, we did. . . . When I saw you two coming up the walk, I thought Keats was one of our prospective students, looking over the campus."

I was in shock.

Keats said, "Will the girls be able to come here?"

"When one gets into Sevens, yes, or as a visitor of a Sevens."

"Oh no!" I groaned. "Girls in Sevens!"

Keats gave me a look. "And what's wrong with that?"

"I just can't imagine it."

"I thought you were a little brighter than that."

Mrs. Violet said, "So did I, Fell. You are, too."

"Some sexist pigs are bright," said Keats, "but they lack emotional maturity."

"Don't gang up on me," I said.

"Oh, poor baby," said Keats.

Mrs. Violet was laughing. "You'll get used to the idea, Fell," she said.

She just assumed I was coming back. If I didn't, I supposed there'd be those who'd imagine it was because females were finally going to be a part of life at The Hill. Gardner'd gone coed. I tried to picture them there, but nothing would come through in focus.

I finally got around to showing Keats my suite, which was what had brought us to Sevens House.

If you've made a decision not to return, we must know immediately, Fell, the headmaster'd written just last week. *And, of course, you must alert Sevens.*

The place had the eerie look of some dead person's rooms whose loved ones had decided to keep just as he left them.

There was the Smith-Corona word processor Dib and I had bought together. There was a photograph on my desk of me dressed up as Sevens' founder, Damon Charles. I'd gone to The Charles Dance that way—every male attended as someone named Charles. I'd caught a lot of flak because it was disrespectful to dare to pose as him.

There were a few bottles of Soho lemon spritzer on the windowsill, and the jacket to my tan gabardine suit on the back of the desk chair.

And there, between a history of the downfall of the Roman empire and a Paul Zindel novel, was the little black folder, with the fleur-de-lys stamped on it in gold. Inside, Delia's letters with the Switzerland postmark, a paper napkin from The Surf Club in The Hamptons, a newspaper photo of her in Zurich, in a raincoat, a scarf around her long black hair, a cigarette burning. . . . Delia: the antidote to Keats, the one who'd "pulled me out in time," as Paul McCartney used to sing in one song. . . . A year later what I needed was the antidote to Delia.

18/FELL DOWN

I wondered where she was and if she ever thought about me. And I thought then what I couldn't get out of my head all summer: Dib had never even been with a girl, except that first time at Willing Wanda's. He hadn't had a clue to what it was all about.

Behind me, Keats said, "You guys are really spoiled! I live in one room half the size of this one."

"I wonder if I could ever come back here."

"You mean because it's coed?"

"I don't know what I mean," I said. But I did. I meant could I ever be the old John Fell again? I'd lied when I'd told Keats I was through blaming myself for what happened to Dib. That was like saying you'd gotten the mildew off something . . . and maybe you had. But it'd be back.

I couldn't shake the idea that if only I'd spent a little more time with him, he wouldn't have turned to Little Jack . . . and after he finally did, I was still too busy being a Sevens, and being me: self-absorbed, and self-important.

"It's too hot up here," Keats said. "I think I should go and check into that Howard Johnson's we saw coming into Cottersville. Obviously, you can stay here after all."

We hadn't been certain that Sevens House would be open.

I could remember the day when, given this situation, I'd be scheming to be in the same place she was that night.

Instead, I told her "Most girls stay at The Cottersville

Inn right in town."

"Then I'll check in there. You should pack some of your stuff up . . . and maybe call Little Jack, hmmm?"

She was standing in front of the window. I could see The Tower in the distance, where the Sevens clubhouse was. I remembered standing at the top of that thing that night I was asked to join. I remembered The Sevens serenading me down below:

The time will come as the years go by,
When my heart will thrill
At the thought of The Hill,
And the Sevens who came
With their bold cry,
WELCOME TO SEVENS, I
Remember the cry.
WELCOME TO SEVENS!

"What'll you do this afternoon?" I asked Keats.

"Shop," she said.

I had a sudden vision of girls streaming down from The Hill after classes, on their way into Cottersville to shop.

I walked Keats out the door, but she held up her hand as I tried to see her down the stairs and out the front.

"No, Fell, you get as much done as you can. I'll be back for you around six."

"Don't snack," I said. "I know a great place we can get some lobsters. My treat."

"This is funny, isn't it, Fell?" Keats said.

"What do you mean?"

"Remember us? Can you imagine lobster being the highlight of our evening back then?"

"Was it escargots? Shrimp? I don't recall."

She gave my arm a punch. Then she leaned into me and kissed me. "Remember now?" she said.

"Of course! It was sauteed eel."

She blew me another kiss as she walked away from me. I smiled at the idea both of us were thinking the same thing about the night ahead of us: how far we'd come from the time we couldn't keep our hands off each other . . . when we'd named the backseat of my car "The Magnet" . . . and when we kept making our dates earlier because we couldn't wait.

"Fell?" Keats called at me from downstairs. "It'll be more like seven. I want to shop for shoes out at the mall."

▣

As it turned out, she was waiting outside in her little baby-blue Benz at quarter after six, top down.

It wasn't my treat, either . . . wasn't fish, but ribs charcoaled on an outside grill.

We dined at a long redwood picnic table, covered with a blue-and-white-checked cloth.

We were in the backyard of 11 Acquetong Road, home of the Horners, Tom and Lucy and Little Jack.

We'd been invited to Little Jack's birthday party, but it seemed we were to celebrate without him.

2
THE MOUTH

Oh, the excitement (the rapture, really) of meeting your other! Can you imagine what that would be like?

Neither could they, of course, because neither one knew he was meeting someone on that bus who would change him forever.

Life is mysterious, you know, or we'd have some clue as to what we're all doing here.

"Is this seat taken?" he asked.

"Help yourself."

"I'm Nels Plummer."

"Leonard Tralastski. Hi!"

He sat beside Lenny on the aisle seat of the Gardner bus. Everything about him seemed to be the opposite of Lenny.

Lenny was tall, dark, black haired, and brown eyed

behind the thick glasses he could not see without. He had a plain, average sixteen-year-old face, regular features, no ethnic imprint.

Nels, same age, was short, light skinned, and blue eyed. He had one of those round, angelic faces, and angel hair, too, golden and curled. He wore a little slanted grin most of the time, but it wasn't particularly warm or friendly.

Lenny's clothes were picked out and bought at Macy's with an employee's discount, by his mother.

Nels' came from Brooks Brothers after he deliberated over them for a long time.

Lenny had on a brown suit and a wool tie.

Nels would not have worn either thing, not ever!

As they began talking, they discovered three things immediately.

1. About the same time Lenny's father was dying a World War II hero, Nels' mother was dying in childbirth. Then that summer past, Nels' father died, too. Poor little tyke was alone in the world . . . almost . . . *almost*. (*Presque*, as they say in Paris; and in Madrid they say *casi*. See how many languages you can say "almost" in.)

"All I have is this older sister, but she's too busy working," said Nels.

"All I have is my mother, and she's too busy working, too," said Lenny.

2. Lenny was the big reader, but the smart one was Nels, who claimed he read only Swinburne.

"Who?" said Lenny.

"He's a poet."

"I must have missed him," said Lenny, who never read poetry except for kinky stuff: *HOWL!* or Leonard Cohen.

3. Neither boy had a big collection of friends back home . . ."or even one," Nels admitted.

▣

If Nels was comfortable being friendless, Lenny wasn't. He made excuses for himself. He said how sick he'd been as a kid, how he'd invented Handy as a result and become fascinated by ventriloquism.

Nels groaned. "Remember I told you I had a sister?"

"Yes. Annette."

"She's adopted. They adopted her because they didn't think they could have children. . . . Then guess what."

"You came along."

"Right, Lenny. Out of the blue, a mortal surprise to my mother. . . . But before I made my appearance, Annette was spending most of her time in bed. She was always sick with something. That's how Celeste came into the picture."

"Who's Celeste?"

"My sister's dummy. My father had it made for her. She was this big deal in our house when I was growing up."

"Is she wooden?"

"Wooden. Red wig. She's like another sister, Lenny. You see, Annette is a *real* ventriloquist. A professional. She's considered very good, I guess."

"I'd love to see her."

"She works for Star Cruises aboard the *Seastar*."

"Neat!"

"Except for the fact that I hate that little tree stump of hers!"

Lenny looked at him to see if there was a possibility he was serious. He was.

He said, "Celeste had her own room when I was growing up, and more toys than I had. . . . Now my sister's a fat pig because of her. You should have seen Annette when I was little, Lenny. She could have been a movie star!"

"How could Celeste make her fat?"

"She wanted her that way."

"Are you kidding?"

"She'd open this ugly little red mouth and whine: *Tick tock tickers! Where's my Snickers?* That's her favorite food. Snickers bars."

"I suppose Annette had nothing to do with it."

"Oh, sure, Annette's partly to blame."

Lenny said to himself: Partly.

Nels said, "My sister is always on this seafood diet."

"You can't get that fat eating seafood."

"On my sister's seafood diet she sees food and eats it."

Lenny laughed, but he was thinking, He's not kidding about the dummy doing that to his sister, is he?

囗

The school was coming into view.

It was at the top of a big hill.

Lenny said once that it "loomed" at you just as you

rounded a bend and saw the city sign: COTTERSVILLE.

The bus was met by a dozen boys in light-blue blazers and navy-blue pants.

All the blazers had gold 7's over the blue-and-white Gardner insignias.

Nels raised an eyebrow in a cynical expression as he looked out the window at them and back at Lenny.

The group began to form a seven, all the while singing:

Others will fill our places,
Dressed in the old light blue.
We'll recollect our races.
We'll to the flag be true.

And . . . da da dee da da dee—I can never remember the words, but Lenny got to know them by heart. He loved that song as much as Nels didn't.

Nels made up some vile verses of his own, so irreverent only he'd sing them.

Anyway, as they walked down the aisle of the bus, Nels asked, "What's the seven supposed to mean?"

"Search me," Lenny said.

"Well, it must mean *something*," said Nels.

(You better believe it, Big Guy.)

3

Lucy Horner made spareribs that fell off the bone when you touched them with a fork. She made fresh applesauce from the apple trees in the yard. Potato salad with hard-boiled eggs in it.

After she'd served us this double-layer fudge cake with a butter icing, I was mellowed out on home cooking and into a soaring chocolate high.

They could have convinced me of anything, even that Little Jack was innocent.

Innocent . . . heartsick . . . and don't forget: eager to contact me.

I told Mr. Horner that if his son had been all that eager, it would have been as simple as picking up the phone.

"He wanted to. He couldn't."

"I tried to stop him from driving that day," I said, "but he laughed and called me Felly."

"He wanted very badly to see you. He still does."

"What for? To say he's sorry he was bombed?" I wanted to rub it in that Little Jack had been drinking. Somebody had to admit that. The police must have known. Maybe the Horners didn't.

But they did. Mr. Horner's eyes looked past me to some safer place in the distance.

He said, "I think the two of them had a fight in that car, and I wouldn't be surprised if it had been about Jack's drinking."

"He hasn't touched a drop since," said Mrs. Horner. She was taking the candles out of the birthday cake to save, same as my mother'd save them for the next cake. When she'd come out with the cake inscribed HAPPY SEVENTEENTH BIRTHDAY, JACK! she'd made some apologetic noises about it being his favorite cake, and even though he wasn't there it wouldn't seem like his birthday if she didn't bake it.

She had these big brown eyes, and a cherubic face framed by mounds of tangled hair.

I felt sorry for her, not sorry enough to join her in singing "Happy Birthday," as Keats did . . . but sorry a woman like that had to be stuck with such a son.

"Says he'll never drink again," Mr. Horner said.

I don't know why they both sounded as though that was some kind of major accomplishment. He was several years away from the legal drinking age.

I wanted to get back to the alleged fight. I asked Mr.

Horner why he thought there'd been one.

"Jack was crying one night and—"

"Crying his eyes out," Mrs. Horner interrupted. "I've never seen our son weep that way."

"He could hardly talk, but he did manage to get out that the last words he said to Dib were *Shut up!*"

"Dib must have been reminding him he had one DWI and if he got another he'd be in big trouble. That's what I think," said Mrs. Horner.

I jumped right in at that point. "But apparently he *didn't* get in big trouble."

"Fell, Jack was run into. That old Cadillac crossed the line and rammed into Jack."

I couldn't really give either one of them a hard time. It was as though Central Casting had picked them to be The Nice Parents. . . . He even smoked a pipe, which gave him a sort of philosophical air: the thoughtful type. A pharmacist by profession, you could imagine him ministering to people, wearing one of those short white coats people wear who can't have the long one that means MD.

"We're not proud of what happened," Mrs. Horner said.

"We're not ashamed of it, either," her husband said defensively. "Jack didn't murder anyone, by design or by accident. Jack's a victim too."

"Well . . ." said Mrs. Horner.

"Well *what*? He is!"

"Well, he didn't get charged for driving while drinking. We should be very grateful for that."

He shot her a look.

Then he sighed, and by his posture seemed to cave in with relief that someone was finally saying what had been unspoken all evening. He stretched his legs out in front of him, ran his hand through his thinning hair, and sighed again.

"In a small town, people are family," he said.

She said, "If Mrs. Greenwald, across the street, has a migraine and late at night needs something strong to get her out of pain, Tom's not going to tell her sorry, you have no prescription."

Keats was nodding in agreement and sympathy.

"The authorities knew Jackie had that one DWI, and his license was suspended. . . . He could have been in real trouble."

"He's never going to drive again, either. Never! That's what he says," Mrs. Horner said.

"That's what he says now," said Mr. Horner.

"I'm glad he's not driving this weekend, with all the drinking that'll be going on there."

"I doubt there'll be drinking," he said.

"What kind of a convention doesn't have plenty of drinking?" she said.

He said, "Jack's at a ventriloquists' convention."

"The fellow driving the car? Ever hear of Lenny Last?" Mrs. Horner said.

Keats snapped a finger. "Of course! Now I remember! Lenny Last and Plumsie!"

"He was a ventriloquist," Mr. Horner said. "I never heard of him."

"I heard of him and I saw him!" Mrs. Horner said. "He was on *The Tonight Show* once, and I saw him on an afternoon show, too."

"Anyway, that's where Jack's heading tonight. He's going to a convention and selling the dummy," said Mr. Horner.

"How did he get the dummy?" Keats asked before I could.

"It seems Lenny Last was alive for a while," Mrs. Horner said. "He spoke to my son. He said, 'Please take care of the dummy for me.' That's why I feel so bad about what Jack's doing."

I helped myself to another piece of the cake. It was the real thing, made from scratch, not the airy fluff that you opened a box, added an egg to, and then baked.

"He's doing the only sensible thing," said Tom Horner. "How do you take care of a dummy? You turn it over to someone who knows how to pull its strings."

"Tom, it doesn't have strings. It's not a puppet."

He ignored the correction and turned back to me. "This fellow Last had only one relative: his mother. She's in a home in upstate New York. I called her to offer my help, and she asked me to place a death notice in *The New York Times*. She put everything but his hat size in it, said she didn't care that it'd cost an arm and a leg. And I helped her get the body up there, too. Who was going to do it all if I didn't?"

"Tom did everything he could for the old lady."

"She had no quarrel with the idea that Jack keeps

the dummy. She seemed relieved, if you ask me."

"Then our telephone began to ring off the hook," said Mrs. Horner. "This fellow was eager to buy the dummy."

"Are you too young to remember Charlie McCarthy?"

"I've seen him in old movies," I said. "He always wore a tux and a top hat, and the ventriloquist's lips moved."

"Edgar Bergen and Charlie McCarthy," Keats said. "Sure. Edgar Bergen was Candy Bergen's father."

"The same men who made Charlie made Plumsie," said Mr. Horner.

"They were brothers," she said. "The McElroy brothers. I remember the name because we've got McElroys for neighbors."

"This fellow trying to buy the dummy is up to a thousand dollars now. One thousand dollars!"

"That's why Jack went out to The Hamptons. He thinks the dummy's probably worth a lot more."

I was waiting for Keats to squeal, *The Hamptons!*

Mrs. Horner said, "But he did the dumbest thing of all. He forgot Plumsie's suitcase. Called us last night—"

Then it came. "The *Hamptons*? That's where I live!"

"You're kidding, Kates!" Mrs. Horner just couldn't get the name right.

"Keats will be heading there tomorrow," I said.

"There's a God in heaven!" said Mrs. Horner. "Do you know a place called Kingdom By The Sea?"

"Cap Marr's place, sure," said Keats. "Everything there is named after a poem by Edgar Allan Poe."

"And the rooms don't have numbers, they have names. Jack's in one called 'The Raven.'" Mr. Horner's face was wrinkled up suspiciously. I didn't figure him for a poetry lover.

Keats laughed. "Yes, that's the place, all right. It's very romantic. There's a big fountain in the courtyard. Cap Marr's dead wife was supposed to be related to Poe. . . . Last year they had a convention of numerologists."

I'd never heard any of it. I'd only lived in Seaville under two years. But I remembered the place. It was outside of Amagansett, a huge structure that rambled on behind the ocean dunes. Last time I'd seen it, it looked like an old, abandoned amusement park.

"Would you take the suitcase to Jack?" Mrs. Horner asked Keats. "It's got a whole wardrobe for the dummy inside. The convention begins tomorrow and runs to Monday."

"Fell?" Keats looked at me. "Will you be finished by tomorrow? Would you come with me?"

"It sounds good to me, sure." It sounded better than work. It sounded better than responsibility.

"Jack thinks he can get a better price if he's got all Plumsie's clothes. They're very fancy duds, Jack says."

"I would love to peek in on a ventriloquists' convention," said Keats. "I can't think of anything more bizarre."

"And that'll give Jack the chance to talk with you,

Fell," Mr. Horner said. "I think he wants you to know exactly how the accident happened."

And how it went unreported that Jack was drunk, with a suspended license for one DWI already—sure. Jack wanted to fill me in on all that.

But I was full of good food and pleasant summer-night-backyard vibes. It wasn't the Horners' fault they loved their son.

Keats and Mrs. Horner rambled on as they went in to get Plumsie's things. I watched some bumblebees duck inside a red rose, leaned back, shut my eyes, and almost forgot Mr. Horner was across from me.

I sat up and glanced over at him.

He'd been watching me, I think. He looked away and back, shaking his head. Then he said, "I thought you'd be a lot more interested in all of this than you are, Fell."

"Why is that, sir?"

"Oh, never mind the sir. . . . I wish my boy had picked up some of that Hill polish. I guess being a day student is different."

"Yes, it's hard to be a townie at Gardner."

"And of course you're in the famous Sevens club."

"How did you know that?"

"I remember Jack telling me that Dib's best friend was a Sevens. That's you, isn't it?"

"That's me."

"It's why I thought you'd be more enthusiastic about all this involvement my boy's had with Lenny Last. He was the last one to speak to him . . . and now he's got the dummy."

"I don't get it, Mr. Horner. What's the connection with Sevens?"

"Why, he was a Sevens, Fell!"

"Are you sure, Mr. Horner?"

"He was staying at your residence."

"That wasn't mentioned in *The Compass*."

"I noticed. We protect our own. You protect your own. It wasn't even mentioned that he was visiting Gardner. I guess Sevens *and* the school just can't take any more bad publicity . . . But I sent some drugs to him there. Asthma medicine, and a little Valium. A Mrs. Violet signed for them."

"During Easter vacation?"

"That's right, Fell. And when he left . . . there was the accident. That same day."

"I didn't know," I said.

"I've always been curious about the club. . . . The things you hear, sometimes it's hard to believe."

"Like what?"

"Oh, you know the things. That you take care of your own throughout a lifetime. That you live all over the world, and you keep in touch . . . the rewards . . . The Revenge."

I knew he was going to get around to that.

"I think The Sevens Revenge is more myth than reality," I said.

"Oh, Fell, I'm not trying to pin you down. . . . You should be proud of yourself. You must have done something good to get in with that group."

That's what everybody thought. If they only knew I hadn't done anything but name a tree something with seven letters in it.

It was the great secret of Sevens, known only to its members.

We'd gotten in by mere chance.

Keats was carrying the suitcase when she came back with Mrs. Horner. It looked like the little cowhide carry-on my mom had ordered from the Sharper Image catalog for me.

I reached for the bag, and we thanked them for dinner.

"Fell?" said Mr. Horner. "Will you do me a favor? Will you let Jack talk to you before you say anything to him? He's just a kid. He doesn't have that Sevens polish."

Keats gave me a poke in the ribs, grinning. "Not like Fell, hmmm?" she said to them.

The one sure thing to break Keats up was the idea I was cool. She'd known me from way back when I was wrestling wheels of cheese after school, in Plain and Fancy, then tooling up the long drive to her palatial home, my old 1977 Dodge Dart backfiring to announce me.

We stuck Plumsie's suitcase in the trunk of the Benz and waved good-bye to the Horners.

Keats asked me to drive. She was tired.

"I'm so excited, Fell! To think you're going to be upstairs in Adieu again . . . this time with Daddy's permission."

Her father had named their house Adieu, because it was the last one he would ever design before his retirement.

I could see her father's face very clearly, the grimace after he'd asked me what *my* father did for a living and I'd said he was a detective.

"*Was?*" he said. "Is he dead?" He made it sound very déclassé to be fatherless.

I didn't have the right stuff for Keats' crowd, only for Keats herself, and that was enough to blackball me forever.

"I think I'd better sleep on the beach," I said.

"No. I think Daddy likes you now that he knows we're not involved that way anymore."

"To me, that's more bizarre than a ventriloquists' convention: keeping Daddy posted when you're not involved that way anymore."

"We're a very close family," she said.

I said, "Don't."

"Don't what?"

"Remind me of close families," I said. "My mother's starting to date and I hate it!"

She reached over and messed up my hair. "Fell," she said, "you're so available when you're down. . . . It's nice."

3
THE MOUTH

Nels said, "What's the seven supposed to mean?"

"Search me," Lenny said.

"Well, it must mean *something*," said Nels.

"I wonder if they assign roommates or what," said Lenny.

"If not, I'm your man," said Nels.

▣

In no time at all Plummer/Tralastski was on the nameplate in 2B, South Dormitory. (Or was it 3B? I never can remember.)

No one at Gardner could help being impressed by The Sevens, except Nels. Lenny wanted to think that his new best friend was just putting on an act. They couldn't be that far apart in what they liked and what they didn't, and Lenny admired The Sevens. They had such style.

"If you're after style," Nels told him, "throw out that orlon sweater. Never wear any clothes made out of petroleum—only fibers made by sheep, plants, or worms."

"You can afford that. I can't," Lenny complained.

Nels had shoes that cost five hundred dollars each. Not each pair. Each foot.

They were John Loeb hand-made reversed waxed calf.

"But that's not style," said Nels. "That's extravagance. That's what I learned at my father's knee."

"What did he do for a living?" Lenny asked him.

"What I'm going to do, probably. Inherit."

▣

One November day, near twilight, seven of The Sevens cornered Nels as he was coming from track.

He was in shorts and an old T-shirt, the sweat on his body just beginning to turn cold.

Nels thought he was in for some kind of new-boy harassment from The Sevens. Apparently they were in charge of whatever hazing there was at Gardner. New boys had been warned that they were to have memorized as many seven things that went together as they could.

Nels liked to stroll around their room while Lenny was studying, pretending to practice for this very moment. He'd say, "Let's see: ca-ca, shit, merde, poop, feces, turd, number two.

"And, let's see: pee-pee, tinkle, wee-wee—"

"SHUT UP!" Lenny would holler.

□

"Sevens!" a senior shouted at him.

Nels named the seven wonders of the world.

But in between the Pyramids of Egypt, and the Tomb of Mausolus, as he faced the steely-eyed, self-assured Sevens who'd barked the order, Nels thought, Dog-Breath, you stink! And after the Pharos of Alexandria, before the Hanging Gardens of Babylon, Nels thought, When you go home, throw your mother a bone.

He told Lenny that was how he got through it.

Once he was one of them, he said to the same senior, "I hope this isn't going to conflict with my membership in the Book-of-the-Month club."

The senior roared with laughter.

What a joker! . . . Right?

□

Across campus, the lights were just going on.

There, on a pathway near the library, another confrontation was taking place.

"Sevens!" a senior shouted at Leonard Tralastski.

Lenny named the seven hills on which Rome was built.

Soon, members of Sevens in both locations appeared with lighted candles, singing.

Singing Plummer and Tralastski into the most privileged organization there . . . and, some thought, *anywhere*.

40/FELL DOWN

For a while the reason was not clear to them, particularly since their backgrounds were so different, and particularly because they were the only two new members admitted that year. Why just the two of them?

It was weeks before they were told the truth, the same day they were moved into suites across the hall from each other, in Sevens House.

They had both almost forgotten all about a tree-planting ceremony after they got off the bus that first afternoon.

But they did remember how they laughed, later, when they found out each one unbeknownst to the other had chosen to name the tree after one of its relatives: Celeste.

4

"Packing up, Fell?"

"Just a few suits, Mrs. Violet. I'll be back for the rest if I decide not to stay on."

"I hope you decide to stay."

"Thanks. I'm glad you're still up. I wanted to ask you something."

It was ten thirty when I dropped off Keats at the inn. She was too tired to take me back to The Hill, so I'd borrowed the Benz. I'd seen only one dim light on in Mrs. Violet's suite. I figured she was probably tucked in with the TV on.

But no—she was bright-eyed and high-heeled, and she said she'd just gotten in herself. She thought she'd see how I was coming along. I had an idea she thought she'd see if I'd invited Keats back for the night, which was against the rules. Even though we were supposed to be self-governing, Mrs. Violet always seemed to know everything that was going on.

"What did you want to ask me, Fell?"

While I told her about the evening at the Horners', and asked her what she could tell me about Lenny Last, she came all the way into the suite and sat down on the couch.

"Yes, he was here," she said. "He stayed in the guest suite for a few days."

"Did you talk with him?"

"Far more than I cared to. Every time I came out of my door, there he sat in the reception area, chain-smoking his Kent cigarettes and wheezing. He had very bad asthma."

"And the dummy?"

"Was locked in the car. Plumsie he called him, sometimes just Plum . . . and he never called him a dummy. He said Plumsie insisted on being called a figure. That's when I knew I had very little to say to the man. . . . Do you have any instant coffee, Fell?"

"Sure!" I got up and went across to plug in the hot plate. "No milk, though," I said.

"I take it black."

"Did he just hang around here by himself?"

"Here and in the video stores. He was looking for an old film called *I Love Las Vegas*. He said it'd inspired him to become a professional ventriloquist. He said Elvis had a cameo role in it."

"I'd like to see it myself. I'm curious now."

"*Now?* You're always curious, Fell."

"So you never saw the dummy?"

"I began to think it was alive. He bought candy for it! Can you believe that? A certain candy bar—the name skips my mind right now."

"Are you kidding me?"

"No, Fell, I'm not."

I was jabbing a fork inside a jar of Taster's Choice to try and chip away a teaspoon of the stuff. The coffee'd been sitting in the sun on my windowsill.

"Never mind," she said.

"I'm getting some, just be patient."

"I don't feel like it anymore. It's too hot up here."

I put down the jar and unplugged the hot plate.

Mrs. Violet uncrossed her long legs and stretched. "I'm tired, too. . . . You know, he wasn't called Lenny Last when he was on The Hill. He was Leonard Tralastski. And he was best friends with the mysterious Nels Plummer."

Nels Plummer was sort of a minor legend at Gardner, and particularly in Sevens. He was like James Hoffa, or Judge Crater, or Etan Patz. One day he'd just disappeared.

She said, "There's a writer named Tobias who's fascinated with missing people. He calls here sometimes, still. He called after Lenny Last's death notice appeared in *The Times*. He thought I was the old housemother and he started in saying Mrs. Kropper, you know what I want: I want to hear the account of the accident in *The Cottersville Compass*."

Mrs. Violet was standing, ready to leave. She said, "Apparently Lenny Last made a habit of coming back here from time to time. He told me everything started here for him. I said you mean being a ventriloquist? He said no, the whole *miesse meshina*. I didn't know what that meant and he said it's Yiddish; it rhymes with Lisa Farina, and it means wretched Fate. I liked that, and I wrote it down. . . . Then he laughed and said he was exaggerating. He said what he meant was he came into his own here. I'll never forget what he said next."

"What?"

"He said that the best was right here, that after this nothing could ever measure up."

That had a familiar ring. I'd heard a few old grads say the same thing.

"I guess he went downhill after he graduated," said Mrs. Violet. "He didn't look too successful. He had nice clothes but he was driving that old boat of a white Cadillac."

"Some people prize those old cars."

"He was wheezing and coughing so much and he smelled of liquor. I bet Mrs. Kropper liked that a lot," she said sarcastically. "She was such an old biddy. . . . But he said they got along famously. He said she'd known them both: Plummer and him."

"Plumsie must have been named for Plummer."

"You know, I never thought of that, Fell."

"Didn't this Tobias write a book about Nels Plummer?"

"He wrote a book about four famous missing people. Plummer was one of the four."

"Famous, I guess, because he was rich."

Mrs. Violet nodded. "Tobias claims the two boys were fast friends and may have had a fight right before Plummer's disappearance. Do you know anything about all of that?"

"I wasn't even born," I said.

"Don't be cruel," Mrs. Violet said.

She walked over to the door. "There was something else, too. He couldn't get over my first name."

"Which is?"

"Laura."

"Laura Violet. Nice."

"But Laura isn't all that rare a name, Fell. He said he'd known someone named Laura, and wasn't that odd that it was my name, too? I didn't think it was so odd."

"I don't either."

"But he went on and on about it, as though it was some kind of omen. '*Really?*' he said. 'How extraordinary! A dear, dear friend of mine was named Laura. Now she's a shrink in Philadelphia. I haven't seen her for years!'. . . He made so much of it, Fell. Perhaps he was just very lonely. He said my name took him on a little trip down Memory Lane."

"He talked that way?"

"There's nothing wrong with that."

"It's pretty corny."

"As you get older, the corn gets dearer." She gave

me a little farewell salute. "Come back this fall, Fell."

I said, "We'll see."

As soon as she left, I finished packing.

What did I care about Last or Plummer? One was History, the other Ancient History. I had the clothes I'd come for, and Fate had arranged a meeting for me with Little Jack.

Laura Violet poked her head back inside the door. "The candy bars Plumsie likes are Snickers, Fell. . . . Maybe you should take him some," and she snickered herself.

4

THE MOUTH

In tennis love means zero and in Sanskrit it means trembling elbows.

It surprised Lenny how fast and how much Nels liked him.

Adored him, truly. Zero . . .Trembling elbows.

Lenny had never been adored by anyone but his mother, who was so busy working so he could have things, that he never had enough of her.

Now there was someone always there for him.

And that someone was not ordinary, nor was the time they spent together ever predictable or dull.

Nels taught Lenny about sex and psychoanalysis. His father had hired people to introduce him to both, said Nels.

Nels liked Republicans, and Lenny Democrats. They

pushed their politics at each other ardently, both night owls who liked to stay up to study and argue and eat.

While Lenny went out for the drama club, Nels threw himself into debating, and made the Gardner team. . . . When Lenny danced and sang a lead role in *The Sound of Music*, Nels' argument for invading Cuba "now!" put his team over the top against Groton.

Of the pair, it was Nels who could express affection, and Lenny who didn't know how.

Lenny wished he could be more relaxed and accepting.

Instead, he would cringe down the school hall when Nels called out, "Hey, Lover-Boy, wait up!"

He would jump when Nels took his arm under an umbrella.

He would suffer, get red, and then ask Nels, "What's this thing you have about acting like a fairy when people are watching us?"

"A fairy wouldn't dare act as I do, Lenny."

"I guess not. . . . You have to realize that my mother and I only kiss at birthdays or at bus and train stations."

"My father always said he'd die young, so we'd better get our hugs in. Plummer males don't live long. I won't, either! . . . Annette learned from Daddy. She hugged me and kissed me and told me she loved me every day. Of course, she told Celeste the same damn thing. I'd hear her in Celeste's room cooing at her, promising her this and that, and that little witch would make fun of it."

"Yeah, yeah," said Lenny, who had no patience with his crazy talk about Celeste.

Sometimes Nels would come running quietly from a long distance and hop on Lenny's back, hook his legs and arms around Lenny, and say playfully, "Giddyap, horsie! Your master wants a ride!"

Lenny was miserable if it was in Sevens House and others saw. He'd try to look as though he wasn't miserable, but he blushed so easily, and then as his face got hot, so did his temper, and it showed in his features he hated Nels doing that. Any minute he'd expect someone to crack the wrong kind of joke, but The Sevens loved Nels.

His aweless approach to their sacred club was unique.

They'd ask themselves, What would impress a Nels Plummer?

No. Wait. They wouldn't say "a Nels Plummer" as though there was more than one.

They'd ask themselves, What would impress Nels Plummer?

There was only one Nels.

□

I'll tell you someone who impressed our boy. Algernon Charles Swinburne. (Never heard of him, right?)

This twisted poet of yore (a lush, yes; none of them are ever happy) inspired Nels to underline so many passages!

One afternoon Lenny took a good look at what it was that captured his pal's attention.

———

50/FELL DOWN

I wished we were dead together today,
Lost sight of, hidden away out of sight,
Clasped and clothed in the cloven clay,
Out of the world's way, out of the light.

Oh, yes . . . and how about this one?

At the door of life, by the gate of breath,
There are worse things waiting for men than death.

Sick, sick sick . . . and he was all Lenny's.

5

My five-year-old sister answered the phone and told the operator she'd accept the charges.

I thought the operator'd tell her to ask an adult if it was all right, but the operator didn't pay the phone bills.

"Mommy's across the hall with Mr. Lopez," Jazzy said.

"You don't sound happy about it."

"You know what he's doing to her?"

I held my breath. "What?"

"He's taking up the hems on all her skirts!"

I had to laugh or I'd cry. "Well, that's good isn't it? What are boyfriends for, anyway?"

"They're not for that!"

"How do *you* know?"

"Because boys don't sew!"

"But honey, Mr. Lopez is a tailor."

"I know what he is! I hate it!"

"Oh, come on. Boys sew, girls sew—who's to say who's supposed to sew and who isn't?"

"Daddy wouldn't sew. He wouldn't never sew!"

"He *would* never sew."

"That's what I just said, Johnny. When are you coming home?"

"Soon, sweetheart. Go get Mommy."

"Tell her Daddy wouldn't want her going to the movies with Mr. Lopez, Johnny!"

"Jazzy, I know it's hard to get used to, but Mommy has a right to go out. Daddy's in heaven."

"Daddy's not. He's rolling over in his grave."

"What?"

"That's what Aunt Clara said. She said Daddy's probably rolling over in his grave."

Jazzy let the phone drop on the table with a clunk, and I stood waiting, in the phone booth just outside The Tower. It was another hot July morning, and in Bucks County it always felt hotter than anyplace else.

It was ten o'clock on a Saturday. Keats was picking me up in another hour. She liked to sleep in and she liked to take her time dressing.

At least I was back in my clothes—had on a pair of my favorite khakis and an old Depeche Mode T-shirt Jazzy'd picked out for me for Christmas one year. My Sperry topsiders, with my left toe coming through the hole.

When Mom took the phone, she asked me what was so urgent.

"I'm going out to The Hamptons."

"Couldn't you have told Jazzy that?"

"I thought you might want to know the reason."

"I know the reason," Mom said. "You're with *her* and she leads you around like a dog on a leash."

"Mom, Keats and I are just friends now."

Mom made some deprecating noises. She'd never forgive Keats for the time she stood me up on the night of her Senior Prom. Forget the fact it was long gone where I was concerned.

"Well, I guess I'll see you when I get back," I said. I was expecting her to ask me some questions: What *was* the reason? How long would I be away? What about my job? (I figured she could call Le Rêve and tell them I was sick; I'd be back Monday night.)

"Next time don't make me stop everything for something Jazzy could have told me."

"Why, because your seamstress is waiting with beating heart?"

"He's a *tailor*, Johnny, and his beating heart is my business, not yours."

"At least Dad did man's work." I couldn't believe I was saying those things.

"Mr. Lopez does man's work, too—and he doesn't call up his mother to get her to call the place he works and say he's sick. . . . That's what you really want, isn't it?"

"No, that's not what I really want!" My voice croaked in mid sentence, so that I even sounded like a liar. "I didn't even think about that. I had something important to tell you, but you'd rather get back across the hall and have your skirts pinned up!"

There was a pause.

My heart was pounding.

"Oh, Johnny," my mother finally said softly. "What's the matter with us? Oh, honey, I'm sorry."

"I'm sorry, too, Mom."

"Let's start all over, hmmm? Where are you calling from?"

I told her, and I told her all about where I was going and why. But it wasn't an easy conversation. Once you've spit out a lot of venom at each other, it's hard to just get past it.

"Lenny Last, sure," Mom said. "I saw him on *The Tonight Show*, I think. Lenny Last and Plumsie . . . I remember Plumsie called him Tra La, and Lenny got so mad!"

"Why Tra La?"

"How do I know? At first I thought he was singing. You know: Tra la la la. But no. He was calling Lenny that."

"See, Mom, all those years of staying up late waiting for Dad have paid off. You know everything about show business."

I suppose I should have left Dad out of it. I didn't know what was right anymore.

Mom skipped by it and said, "I thought you didn't like this Horner kid. Why go out of your way to see him then?"

FELL DOWN/55

"I don't like *him*. I like his folks. I want to face up to him. . . . I don't even know what I'll say. But I want to put him behind me."

"And you have to go to The Hamptons to do that?" Mom asked. "I hope you're not just running, Johnny. You've got your job now, and it's a good job. They like you there."

"I'm not running," I lied.

I said, "It's better than sitting on a park bench all day, isn't it?"

For a long time I'd done that. I'd gone to the Esplanade in Brooklyn Heights and stared across the river at the New York skyline and out at the Statue of Liberty. I'd thought about jumping in and swimming out until I wouldn't have the breath to make it back.

"Johnny, I love you," Mom said.

"I love you, too," I said. "Will you call Le Rêve for me and tell them I have a very bad case of flu, that I won't be in tonight or tomorrow?"

When I got off the phone, I walked into The Tower. Deem Library was there. The infamous Sevens alumnus David Deem had donated it to the Sevens clubhouse. Before he'd died a mysterious death last spring, he'd fooled everyone. He was your all-around good citizen, owner of a sporting goods store, dutiful father to one daughter and one dachshund. All of Cottersville and Gardner were shocked when he was indicted for dealing drugs.

While he was out on bail, he was shot in his car one

afternoon at twilight, seven times through the heart. There was a dead rat in his mouth, said to be the signature of The Sevens Revenge, the deadly punishment Little Jack's father'd mentioned. It was rumored to be meted out by a Sevens on a member who had disgraced Sevens.

Twilight was a special time for The Sevens. No one really knew why that was, but there were many rituals at twilight and songs with "twilight" in the verse.

I'd known Deem and trusted him. All of that was part of my breakdown, too, and I wasn't eager to hang around in there. What I wanted was to glance at something I knew would be in the library.

It didn't take me long to find his name in the directory, along with the years he'd attended Gardner.

Then from the collection I pulled out the light-blue leather-bound volume with *The Hill Book, 1963* stamped across it in white.

I opened to the P's and there he was: some male version of the old child star Shirley Temple: all curls and dimples, and a big grin.

Nelson Percy Plummer III
New York, New York
Nels . . . Nelly

The Sevens Club, '62, '63.   Debating, '62, '63.

Ambition: To continue as is.
Remembered for: His ego and his alter ego, Tra La.
Slogan: Here's to Swinburne et moi!
Future Occupation: Leader

I flipped a few pages to find Tralastski, who was a serious young man with dark frames on his eyeglasses and his dark hair parted down the middle, lending him an old-fashioned, somewhat scholarly appearance.

Leonard Joseph Tralastski
New York, New York
Lenny . . . Tra La

The Sevens Club, '62, '63.   Drama Club, '62, '63.
Tennis, '63.   Gardner Follies, '63.

Ambition: To be an actor.
Remembered for: Being buddies with Plummer.
Slogan: We three: My echo, my shadow, and Laura.
Future Occupation: Show Biz.

5
THE MOUTH

Not knowing one tiny thing about Sanskrit, I can't *promise* you that love means trembling elbows, so you may feel let down by me. Or question my reliability.

Nels made Lenny feel the same way sometimes.

For example:

One summer day when Lenny was little, his mother took him to Central Park, to escape the heat.

There was a lake in the park. His mother rowed one of the boats out to the middle of it.

"Just think, Leonard," said she, "we wouldn't be here right now if it wasn't for an awful murder."

That was her way of starting the same lesson over again, which she would teach Lenny as long as she drew breath: that if he thought for one minute the rich were happy, *listen!*

FELL DOWN/59

Then she told him of two young men: one filthy rich named Loeb, the other Leopold. Of how they snatched this small boy and murdered him. (It left Lenny terrified of being kidnapped.)

"Why wouldn't we be here if it wasn't for them?" Lenny asked her.

"Because the Loeb family didn't want everyone to remember them for that awful crime a relative committed, so they gave this boathouse to the community."

It was one of the stories Lenny told Nels Plummer, to give him an example of what his mother was like.

Nels used it when he wrote his New Boy's Composition, something required of all entering students.

The theme was "History in Our Daily Lives."

One morning, Sister and I took a boat out on the little lake in Central Park.

"Just think, Nels," said Sister, "we wouldn't be here if there hadn't been a certain violent crime some years ago."

As Nels was reading this to Lenny, Lenny stopped him.

"Very funny!" said Lenny.

"It's not supposed to be funny."

"I ought to know that, since it's my story."

"*Your* story?"

"I told you my mother took me to the park and told me that! Come *on*, Nels!"

"Did you, Lenny? I don't remember that."

"Well, where do you think it came from? Your sister

never took you there and said that."

Nels thought about it. "She could have. We lived right across the street."

"But she *didn't*, Nels!"

"Sometimes I get us all mixed up, Lenny. I don't know where you stop and I begin and vice versa."

"I think you mean it."

"I *do*! I swear I don't remember you telling me that. Don't be mad at Nelly, okay?"

"Do you have to call yourself that?" Lenny asked him.

"My father was called that and his father was, too. It's a proud old name in our family."

"It sounds faggy."

"Not to us. . . . But Celeste always said that Captain Stir-Crazy thought it was faggy, too."

Stir-Crazy was Nels' nickname for the Captain of the *Seastar*. Captain Ian Stirman. Nels didn't like him. Nels didn't like anyone his sister admired.

Jealousy, they say in Hong Kong, comes into the eye as a little yellow freckle.

Nels said, "Stir-Crazy claims that Nelly is what Englishmen call the old ones. Nellies. Why should I care what the English do? Why should he? . . . Unless he's a fag himself."

Lenny wanted to get back to the subject. "Are you going to hand in that essay?"

"I don't have another, Lenny, and it's awfully good. Do you mind?"

"Be my guest, I guess."

"Well, you weren't making use of the incident, were you, in yours?"

Lenny'd written a very dull essay about a trip to the Statue of Liberty. The only people in it were "the French" and "the Americans."

◻

From time to time, Lenny'd catch Nels doing more things like that. He'd made Lenny teach him chess because it was Lenny's favorite game. In no time he played it as though he had for years. Eventually he could beat Lenny, though Lenny knew at times he let Lenny win.

He took on all of Lenny's enthusiasms, forgetting (so he claimed) that they were Lenny's. He'd never even heard of Lenny's favorite poet, Leonard Cohen, never read science-fiction writers like Harlan Ellison, Richard Matheson, or Alfred Bester. He glommed onto them and began finding things in them Lenny hadn't found . . . and of course sometimes he'd recommend something to Lenny that Lenny had told him about.

Sometimes, after one of their bull sessions in Lenny's suite, when they sneaked in a bottle of chianti, Nels would cry, "Toodle-oo to boo-hoo-hoo," which was something Celeste said sometimes in her act, and he'd cross the hall singing Annette's old song to him when he was little: "Seeing Nelly Home."

It was her sign-off, and Celeste would add remarks like "Who *wants* him home?" or "Get *yourself* home next time, jerk!"

Celeste always called Nels "Big Guy."

Nels had a nickname for Lenny, too, but Lenny loathed being called it. Tra La. From Tralastski.

"What's this thing you have against nicknames?" Nels asked him. (Even the expression *What's this thing you have . . .* was Lenny's.)

"I just don't like Tra La," Lenny insisted.

The only other nickname Lenny had ever had he had hated more. It was Wheezy . . . because of his asthma.

Since he had arrived on The Hill, he had not had a single asthma attack.

He attributed that to the clean country air of Cottersville, although there was a tire factory just outside town. Nels claimed it was Nels; Nels said no one ever gave a damn about you before, that's all.

"Tra La and Nelly," said Lenny. "That sounds awful!"

"Agreed," said Nels. "It would sound much better if it were Nelly and Tra La."

A lot of things Nels thought were funny Lenny didn't, at least not right away.

Sometimes not ever.

Tra La not ever.

"How can someone disappear into thin air?" Keats said.

"Someone murders him, or kidnaps him . . . or he decides to begin a new identity."

"He could have amnesia, too," Keats said.

"Maybe we could look the case up on microfilm when we get to East Hampton?"

"No, don't, Fell! Who cares? We're on vacation!"

I didn't feel like heading indoors to stare at microfilm, anyway, that morning. It was the perfect summer day: blue skies and sun above, the green hills rolling by as we left Pennsylvania, top down. Keats was driving.

"I called home and Mummy says she's almost positive Daddy'd want you to spend the week with us."

"Not a week, Keats. A night, two. That's all."

"Fell, you need more time away!"

"What did your mother mean she's 'almost positive'?"

"It means he's not there to ask, but it'll be fine."

"I've got a job, remember?"

"You'd make better tips in Seaville, or in Bridgehampton."

"Wanna bet? I do very well at Le Rêve."

"Good! Because you owe me dinner out somewhere wonderful!" Keats said. "Somewhere they serve enormous lobsters. You whetted my appetite when you promised me that yesterday."

"We'll go to Gosman's in Montauk," I said.

"Let's go early, too, so we can see the sunset and get a table down by the water."

"What if something interesting's going on at the convention tonight?"

"They have to eat dinner, too. We can go there after dinner."

We were making our plans.

Every time I caught myself doing anything fun and familiar, I marked it, telling myself I was back and okay. But I was suspicious of the idea at the same time. If I really was back and okay, how come I was so conscious of it?

Then I'd dip down again for a few seconds. I'd have this picture of myself opening the car door and becoming a big red splatter on the highway.

Keats shoved in an old tape of Tracy Chapman singing her songs of social conscience.

I mumbled something about wondering if a

Mercedes Benz convertible was the ideal place to listen to lyrics about homeless people and police brutality.

"Don't ruin everything, Fell," she said. "Remember that old Billy Joel song—'We Didn't Start the Fire'?"

"We don't have to fan the flame, though," I said, but she turned up the volume.

Why couldn't I just let her be happy?

□

It was late afternoon by the time we hit Seaville. No matter that Brooklyn was my real home, I'd always feel as though I was coming home when I made that right turn at the traffic light and saw the long pond by the road and the graveyard up on the slope. Then the rows of Dutch elm trees and Main Street, with its old white houses and green lawns.

"When I lived here, Kingdom By The Sea was a real dump," I said.

"When you lived here, only the bar was open anymore. But they've remodeled it. Now it's very gothic and spooky. And tacky."

"Mom used to call it The Eyesore, and Jazzy made that into The Ice Store."

There wasn't a lot of traffic as we followed Route 27. It was a perfect beach day. It was the kind of day shopkeepers took chairs out to the sidewalk and sat there reading.

"I'm going to drop you off," Keats said. "I'll give you a few hours and then we'll head for Gosman's."

"I thought you were dying to see a ventriloquists' convention?"

"I am, but I'm also dying to take a bath and change. They'll still be there later tonight, and tomorrow. . . . And you should see Little Jack alone, I think."

"You're the boss."

"No, that's Daddy, who should be home right about now." She took a look at her watch.

I knew then what she was going to do. Beg Daddy to let me stay there.

I said, "I'm not that anxious to be under the same roof with him, either."

"Hush, Fell. Our guest room has a private bath with a sauna, a view of the ocean, and a waterbed."

"I wouldn't mind being under the same roof with him," I said.

"He'll like you, too. Just don't tell him you're suicidal."

"What if he asks?"

She laughed.

She said, "Should I stop at Seaville Video and see if I can find a great film to watch later tonight?"

"See if you can find one called *I Love Las Vegas.*"

"You're kidding, I hope."

"No, I'm not. Lenny Last was hunting for it right before he died. I just wonder why, what's in it."

"You always do this, Fell."

"I always do what?"

"You get too involved . . . in everything."

"Aren't you curious?"

"I'm mildly curious about a lot of things. I'm not consumed with curiosity over every little thing."

"I'm not either."

"Yes, you are. You're like Gras, our new dachshund. If he knows there's anything even remotely resembling food in the room, even an old wadded-up candy wrapper someone's got in his pocket, he roots around and roots around until he finds it."

"Better than your old poodle, Foster. He was a real stuck-up dog."

"He was really Daddy's dog. That's why he didn't take to you."

"Try and get the movie," I said. "Elvis has a cameo role in it."

"I'm not an Elvis fan, either. I think Bruce Springsteen has it all over Elvis."

"Sure, he copied him."

Just when I was beginning to think we'd spent too much time together, and were getting on each other's nerves, Keats said, "Look! There it is!"

It was up on the dunes, a great gold-and-white castle complete with drawbridge, towers, and domed roof.

"I love what they've done to it," said Keats. "It's the tackiest thing I've ever seen in all my life."

"Sure you don't want to come in with me?"

We were crossing the drawbridge.

"No, I've got to get home."

"Don't feel bad if Daddy says no. I can find an old turret in this place to curl up in."

Kingdom By The Sea was right on the dunes, the sea just a short walk away. As we drove up to the entrance, I could feel the wind become cooler and smell the salt air.

Keats stopped the car under an enormous banner flapping in the breeze.

Welcome to the
10th ConVENTion
of American Ventriloquists!
Welcome to Kingdom By The Sea!
Captain Michael Marr, Proprietor

A kid dressed up in sailor's whites came down the steps and asked if we had any luggage.

"A bellboy! I don't believe it," I said.

"A bellperson," said Keats. She handed the sailor the key to the trunk and told him which bag to take.

The sailor hustled inside with it.

"Check out the room situation here," Keats said. "There's a million-in-one chance Daddy'd not be in the mood for company of any kind, nothing to do with you."

"Sweetheart," I said, doing my old Humphrey Bogart imitation, "don't sweat it."

6
THE MOUTH

Ah, The Charles Dance. Of all the events at Gardner School, this was the biggie.

In honor of the Sevens founder, Damon Charles, all males attended the annual Charles Dance as someone named Charles.

Nels was putting together a pilot's outfit to go as Charles Lindbergh, famed aviator and father of a kidnapped child.

"If I was ever going to kidnap," said Nels to Lenny, "I'd do exactly what the Lindbergh kidnapper did—take someone who couldn't talk."

"The Lindbergh kidnapper killed the baby anyway," Lenny said, "so it didn't matter if it could talk or not."

"If I was to suggest kidnapping to you, Tra La, what would you say?"

"I'd say don't call me Tra La."

"Seriously! What would you say?"

"I'd say get some aviator goggles, a silk scarf, or something! You don't look like a flyer, Nels!"

Lenny didn't see any point in talking about kidnapping.

But he remembered the conversation.

One day he would think back to it, and he would remember it very clearly: Yeah, there *was* mention of kidnapping . . . way back that first year.

Nels changed his mind about the Charles he wanted to be, and went to the dance as Charles Ryder, a character out of a novel called *Brideshead Revisited*.

Of course Lenny was going as Charlie McCarthy, of the famous ventriloquist team Edgar Bergen and Charlie McCarthy.

There was another member of Sevens dressed up like the dummy, too.

Nels told Lenny, "Before I'd appear anywhere dressed the same as Carl Delacourt, I'd step into the men's and strip down until I was bare-assed."

Carl Delacourt's head came to a point. His ears stuck out like the handles on a jug. He had mean little feral eyes.

He was a scholarship student like Lenny. The dense and sullen son of an evangelical minister. Diamond, he had named his tree. Diamond? The Sevens asked. He said it was for his idol, for Neil Diamond.

It was well known that Delacourt got furious if anyone brought up the old rumor that Diamond's famous song "Longfellow Serenade" was written to his penis.

Almost anybody would rather put his name on the

blind-date list than bring his sister to a dance as his date.

Not Carl Delacourt.

Right after his name on the Sevens list of Members & Ladies was Delacourt, Laura (Sister).

"She's probably a major wallflower," Nels said while they eyed the list. "Carl says they're both going to be shrinks."

He and Lenny were going stag. You could. It was more fun. It was cheaper, which appealed to Lenny: no corsage to buy. You could play the field, too.

Just as soon as the pair noted that Carl was dressed up as a dummy, and right after their little repartee about it, Laura Delacourt came into view.

"She's not so bad after all," said Nels.

Lenny didn't say anything.

"They couldn't be *blood* relatives," Nels said.

Lenny didn't say anything.

Delacourt and his sister began to dance.

"She moves like an angel and she looks like one," said Angel-Face himself. "I wouldn't mind being shrunk by her."

Silence from Lenny.

"Beauty and the Beast," said Nels.

Lenny didn't say anything.

"Or isn't she your type?" said Nels.

Silence.

"She'd be mine if I liked blonds," said Nels, who would just about come to her shoulder. She was tall and long-legged.

72/FELL DOWN

Then Nels finally turned to Lenny, looked up at him, and said, "Where are you, Tra La?"

For the first time, he saw Lenny's face.

He saw the look in Lenny's eyes as they followed Laura Delacourt in a fox-trot with her ugly brother.

He saw the end of something and he saw the beginning of something.

He felt what he saw like a sock to his insides, but he never showed it.

The old shrug. What would he do without that old shrug to his shoulders?

"Why don't you cut in, Tra La?"

He nudged Lenny with one hand in a halfhearted way.

Still, Lenny couldn't talk. Couldn't move.

Nels didn't push it. Nels wasn't in any hurry to speed this thing along.

A thing like this could change history.

Already had, many times over.

It didn't matter if it was your little destiny it interfered with or the fate of an entire nation.

It left its mark . . . if it ever left.

Lenny finally said something.

"So that's Laura Delacourt."

7

The sailor gave the suitcase to a heavyset fellow at the registration counter. Attached to his dark-blue blazer was a plastic name tag: *Toledo*.

I asked him how I could get in touch with Jack Horner, in The Raven, and he pushed some phone buttons and talked to me while the number rang.

"Is Horner a vent?"

"A what?"

"A ventriloquist?"

"He's here for the convention, yes. You call them vents?"

"They call themselves that," he said. "There's no answer in The Raven."

"Thanks for trying, Mr. Toledo. Would you check the bag, please?"

"Just plain Toledo. . . . Your friend could be at the

Gospel Vents' workshop on the mezzanine, or at Beginners' Tricks down the hall. They're almost over now."

I chose Beginners' Tricks. I went around a corner to French doors opening on a courtyard packed with folding chairs and people sitting in them. . . . People weren't the only occupants, either. There were dummies sitting in some seats. The first thing that struck me was how alike most of the dummies looked, as though they'd all come out of the same mold. Some had different colored wigs, and they were dressed in everything from tuxedos to sailor suits, but they all had those big dark eyes with the wide red mouth and a certain wild-and-crazy-guy expression.

Latecomers were standing in the back.

A skinny, bald guy in a bow tie was pointing to a blackboard where there were four giant letters in white chalk: p, b, m, and f. He called them "the bane of our existence, and the reason for most flapping."

I asked a white-haired man standing next to me what flapping meant.

"Moving your lips," he whispered.

Next the speaker held his hand to his face. It was made up to resemble a tiny head. From the mouth of lipsticked fingers came a shrill little voice saying, "P. B. M. F. . . . Please be my friend."

Everyone clapped.

I tried saying the same words softly to myself, without moving my lips.

Out came *lease e eye wend*.

"How does he do that?" I said.

The man beside me said, "You missed the best part. This is almost over."

While everyone was trying to say the same sentence, I looked at the others. There were a few kids around six or seven and a few my age. There were about a dozen females. The majority were men, all ages. Some had their dummies on their laps.

Jack Horner did.

▣

Little Jack wasn't holding Plumsie as the others held theirs. Plumsie was stretched out on his back, on Jack's bare knees, his eyes staring up at the sky.

Little Jack didn't see me. (I remembered the day he'd called me Felly.)

He had on a black T-shirt and denim shorts, in contrast to Plumsie, who was in a tux with a white shirt, red tie, and red cummerbund. ("Bye-bye, Felly." . . . And Dib's last words to me had been "Cork it, Fell!")

Little Jack was chewing gum, straining to see the speaker past the people in front of him. The sun had bleached his hair the shade of beach sand. He wore it straight, and very long in the back. His tan made his eyes all the more blue.

The speaker's lipsticked fingers opened and the same voice that had begged please be my friend announced the session was over. Part II would begin the next morning at nine.

The man next to me was watching me stare at Little Jack. He didn't look like an Easterner. He had on white pleated pants with a silver buckle on a black belt, a white short-sleeved shirt with silver pocket buttons, and a bolo tie with a turquoise stone.

"So that's how Plumsie ends up," he said. "My, how the mighty have fallen."

I turned to face him. "Did you know Lenny Last?"

"Most of us old-timers did. That's why there was that moment of silence for him at the banquet last night."

"I just got here," I said. "I'm not a vent."

"Your questions told me that." He stuck out his hand. "I'm Guy Lamb," he said. "What are you doing at a vents' convention? Selling something, or buying something?"

"An acquaintance of mine is selling something."

He looked in the direction I was looking. "How'd he get his hands on old Plum?"

"He inherited him from Lenny Last."

"Who is he to Len? Len had only his mother, and she was getting along in years."

I explained that Little Jack had pulled Lenny Last out of the wreck and that Last's dying words were "Please take good care of my dummy."

"That's a lot of bull merde, son."

"That's the story, Mr. Lamb."

"You can call me Guy. . . . That's quite a story. Whoever dreamed up that one didn't know Lenny Last."

"Why do you say that?"

"Len would have never said 'dummy.' That word wasn't in his vocabulary. Particularly when it came to

Plum. And he'd never give Plumsie to a stranger. . . .
We're all attached to our figures, but Lenny was over-
taken by Plum. Some figures do that. They bewitch
their owners."

"Maybe Little Jack misheard him." I had my eye on
Little Jack. Now he was standing with Plumsie caught
between his legs, its face squashed against his calves.

He was lighting up a cigarette, talking to a fellow
who was Asian, tall and twentyish, with a string mustache.

Guy Lamb's mouth was tipped. "Did your friend
mishear Len or did he put words in his mouth?"

"Why would he want a dummy?"

Guy Lamb put his hand on my arm. "Please. Don't
say dummy. Say figure. Say Plumsie. Anything but
dummy."

"A figure," I said. "Why would he want it enough
to lie about it?"

"Why does *anyone* want something enough to lie?
Money, my boy, *dinero.*"

"I don't think Little Jack was thinking about money.
He'd just survived an accident and he was drunk,
too."

"I'd heard *Lenny* was, that it was Lenny's fault,"
said Guy Lamb.

"Was he always a drinker?"

"A big one near the end. Some say it was the gambling debts he was carrying. Others say it was something in his past. Plumsie began remarking about it,
too, as he took over the act, about the drinking *and* the

asthma. That was around the same time he decided he didn't like the name Plumsie."

"What did he want to be called?"

"He never said. What he said was he didn't want a name with seven letters in it, so Lenny started calling him Plum. I think he just liked to irritate Lenny."

I must have made a face without realizing it.

Guy Lamb said, "Sounds farfetched, hmmm? But you should have seen them near the end. Lenny'd wheeze but Plum wouldn't. Lenny'd drink until he slurred before a performance, but Plum never slurred. Then there was this high little voice that would come out of Plum. He'd scold Lenny in it. He'd called Lenny 'Big Guy.' If Lenny fluffed a line, Plum would trill, 'Nice try, Big Guy.' Sometimes with an Italian accent. 'Nice-ah try, Big Guy.' Sometimes it'd be a French accent or German.

"The audience picked up on it, and they'd call out 'Nice-ah try, Big Guy!' Or 'Nice twy, Beeg Guy,'— always in falsetto, like Plum. Some folks thought it wasn't funny, if you know what I mean." He pointed to his ear with one finger, turning it in circles. "Some folks thought Lenny was headed around the bend."

"What was his personal life like?"

"He didn't have one. Lenny was like me, a loner. Now, what went on before I knew him, or inside him— that I can't tell you. Plumsie probably told us more than Len wanted us to know. Some figures will do that, will bring out your devils. My Earl never did, thank the good Lord." He looked over at Little Jack, who was holding Plumsie between his knees while he wrote something down. "Yes," he said, "Lenny was like me. He wanted Plum to end up in The Vent Haven Museum . . . not like that."

"Do you know who Little Jack's talking to?" I asked him.

"Your friend is talking to Fen. He's only been on the scene a few years now, but he's climbing the ladder fast. He played The White House last Christmas."

"Is he Japanese?"

"Vietnamese. Now *he* might be interested in buying Plumsie. He's not too happy with the figure he's got. That's her in the chair behind him. Most vents have figures their same sex, and I expect Fen would be better off with a male himself."

I could see only the back of something about three feet long, all in black with a white wig.

"That's Star," said Guy. "She's got more clothes than a movie star."

"Why do these figures all look alike?" I said.

"They don't. You just don't look carefully. Some look like a lot of others because they're cheapos. Plywood and plastic, stuffed with cotton."

"How much is a cheap one?"

"About five hundred dollars."

"And an expensive one?"

"My Earl upstairs is worth fifteen thousand. Crestadoro made him."

"And Plumsie, what would he go for?"

"Hard to tell. There aren't many like Plumsie anymore. He was made by the McElroys years ago. He probably had a few owners before Len bought him."

"Give a guess," I said.

"Twenty, twenty-five thousand, maybe more. *But* there're not that many collectors interested in figures that expensive, and a professional performer would hesitate to work with him. Plum was too much Lenny's, and he was too strong for Lenny. So he has this undertone. That's what we call it."

"Sort of like a jinx or a curse, hmmm?"

"We call it an undertone," he said emphatically. "Now that Fen fellow wouldn't know enough to be wary of Plum, wouldn't know his history."

"I don't think Little Jack does either, or his worth."

"The blind leading the blind."

"Yeah."

"Of course you're going to enlighten your friend, hmm?"

"I think I'll stay out of it," I said.

Guy Lamb chuckled. "So he's not that close a friend. . . . Good, because I don't like his story about how he got Plum. And it'll be interesting to see if Plum acts up on this Fen."

"How can he, if Fen knows nothing about him?"

"He can, he can. . . . You're a civilian, my boy. That's what we call people who aren't a part of the show-business family. You'd probably whistle in the theater, say the name Macbeth aloud, and wish some poor actor luck, none of which is done. We have our traditions and our customs. We're on the superstitious side.

We favor fancy over fact."

My father used to say the mark of the ignoramus was to poo-poo something just because *you* couldn't imagine it.

"Old Plum will take care of himself," said Guy Lamb. "I'll bet on old Plum any day."

We stood watching while Little Jack picked Plumsie up. He rested it against him face to shoulder, the way someone might hold a small child.

"That's better," Guy Lamb said. "I don't like to see Plum carried around like some stuffed animal won at a carnival for shooting ducks down. He deserves some respect."

That was when Little Jack looked back and spotted me.

It wasn't really a wave he gave me. It was more like a resigned salute.

7
THE MOUTH

And now we come to Laura, or Laura comes to us . . .
and it is summer: *Sommer*, they say in mad Berlin, in
gay Paree *été*. Now Venice, where it's *estate* . . . and in
Sanskrit (truly this time) trembling elbows.

"Poor Nels!" said Laura.

"That's one adjective you can't use in the same
sentence with Nels Plummer," Lenny said.

"But you like him, don't you?"

"You know I more than like him, Laura."

"I worry about him . . . spending the summer alone."

"He could go anywhere, Laura, do anything."

"But who'd he go with, who'd he do it with?"

Good question!

The three of them that summer!

They decided to take jobs at a plush inn in Lake Placid,
New York—the boys waiters, and Laura a waitress.

FELL DOWN/83

They knew while they were doing it how sweet it was, that not much up ahead of them would match the lazy, crazy days from June through August 1962.

One little song like "The Wanderer" or "Ramblin' Rose" would start them off years hence, they all bet on it!

They'd remember the three of them chomping into egg-and-olive sandwiches Laura made on mushy white Buttercup bread, while they floated around on their days off in a Placid Palace rowboat surrounded by the mountain, their skins glistening bronze in the sun while they slathered each other with Coppertone.

Laura could do a good imitation of Barbra Streisand, and she'd sing old revival hymns for them. "Throw Out the Life Line" *(There is a brother whom someone should save)* . . . "Bring Them In" *(Bring them in from the fields of sin)* . . . And "I'll Stand by You 'Til Morning."

She said the way to turn a gospel hymn into blues was to substitute "baby" for "Jesus," and she'd try out her theory with hymns like "Jesus, I Come," and "All for You, Jesus."

They'd skinny-dip by moonlight and at sunrise.

Nels never spent more than he made, and he never once complained about the work. He'd get as excited by a big tip as they would.

The only extravagant thing Nels did all summer was to buy a secondhand white Cadillac for them to get around in. After work, they'd take it across the lake to Smitty's, where they could dance until the stars were fading in the morning sky.

Lenny was in love with his life that summer. In love with Laura, and basking in his loving friend's company.

Nels kept them laughing. He could even make Laura laugh the time a party of ten ordered lobster dinners and walked out without tipping her. It was called "getting stiffed."

Nels' remedy was applied as they sat around a campfire on the beach. He'd made up his hand like a face.

NELS: Good evening, *Hand*some.

HANDSOME: What's good about it?

NELS: Not much. I miss the sun.

HANDSOME: Whose son do you miss?

NELS: S-u-n! Not s-o-n!

Laura was laughing.

"Wait a damn minute, Nels!" Lenny said.

"I know. I know. Some of it is your idea."

"Not some! All!"

"I never saw you do ventriloquism!" Laura said to Lenny. "You just talked about how you used to do it."

"At Sevens House I do. Where do you think Nels got it?"

"I changed the name from Handy to Handsome!" said Nels.

"Big deal!"

"Who cares, Lenny?" Laura said.

Somehow Lenny came off the bad guy for caring.

Laura moved closer to Nels. "What's your sign, Handsome?"

"Sagittarius."

FELL DOWN/85

"Like Nels."

"Just like him."

"That's a fire sign."

Lenny pretended to snore. (He had hated astrology ever since Laura had told him Leo, her sign, and Virgo, his, were not a good combination. Leo would be beaten down by Virgo's tendency to criticize.)

Laura talked above the snoring. "I'm a fire sign too. We're filled with passion, Handsome, not like that earthbound character over there."

"When's your birthday, Beautiful?"

"Tomorrow."

"Tomorrow?" Nels put down his hand, his face suddenly filled with alarm and disbelief. "Why didn't someone tell me?" He was looking straight at Lenny.

Lenny shrugged. "We would have. Tomorrow."

"Too late for me to run out and get Laura the Seven of Diamonds," Nels joked. Of all the jewelry the Sevens purchased for their women, that was the best.

"It's always going to be too late for that," said Lenny sarcastically. "At least where you're concerned."

And Nels looked miffed. "I was just kidding, Tra La. . . . But I do wish someone had said *something*. Aren't we going to have a big birthday party?"

Lenny grabbed Laura's hand. *"We're* going to have a little one."

回

Later, Laura said that Lenny was petty sometimes.

"Poor Nels," she said. "You never let him get out front."

"You're doing it again: calling him *poor* Nels."

"There's something very defenseless about him," Laura said. "He's probably not original enough to dream up his own ventriloquism act."

"I didn't like what he said about it being too late to run out and get you the Seven of Diamonds."

"He was kidding. He said so, Lenny."

"The Seven of Diamonds is only given to fiancées or wives. Where does he get off even kidding about it?"

"First we invite him along with us *all* the time. Then you pull the rug out from under him when he takes anything for granted."

She made Lenny feel bad about how he'd treated Nels. . . . After all, the two of them had a big advantage over Nels that summer. They were the couple.

Lenny encouraged Nels to do Handsome again, but in honor of Laura's birthday, Nels said he wanted to present something original . . . Dr. Fraudulent. His hand had a German accent and a beard made out of fresh corn silk.

"Und zo, Fräulein Laura, vat I hear iss you vant to be a doctor like me?"

"Ja, Herr Doktor, ja!"

"Tell me den, vat iss your darkest secret?"

"I like nice things," said Laura, "beautiful things! But I hate to admit it."

"Vell, I hav here something beaudeefill for you."

It was a thin, 14-karat-gold chain, perfect he said, for a gold 7, someday.

Coincidentally (and because Laura was determined

FELL DOWN/87

to be a shrink), Lenny had given her the collected works of Sigmund Freud. He felt like a jackass for being so unromantic.

◻

Some nights Lenny would see Nels standing by himself at the edge of the dance floor, watching. He would see him ask a girl to dance, only to find that when she stood up, she was even taller than Laura. Nels looked like a little squirt leading her around. He looked like some twelve-year-old kid at a wedding party having to dance with a grown-up.

Lenny's heart broke for his buddy then.

He hated seeing Nels embarrassed, or awkward.

At times, Nels would go off on his own after they came off their shifts. All there really was to do was dance. Nels would wander into town, hang out at the soda shop or the Laundromat, watching for short girls.

Lenny'd lend him a hand, tell him the new young clerk at The Outdoor Store was just about five foot one . . . some other female he'd spotted not an inch over five two. He'd keep a shortie watch out for Nels. So would Laura.

It really didn't matter that much that Nels usually did not have anyone.

They'd sing until they were hoarse and dance in a triangle until the soles of their feet burned.

Maybe times it was just the three of them were the best times, because that was most of the time, and most of the time was better than good.

"Promise that we'll never forget this summer!" Laura

was fond of exclaiming, and they would: They'd promise.

□

At its end Nels gave Lenny the white Cadillac to take back to Gardner.

"We'll have that to remember the summer by," he said, "and Tra La can make some money renting it out."

□

Weekends Laura'd come to see Lenny, they'd zip around Cottersville in it, the three of them squeezed into the front seat.

Little Jack was lighting up.

He smoked Camels. He carried a silver Zippo. He was the only one around in shorts. His baby face, his height, and the shorts made him look even younger than seventeen—more like twelve. People probably wanted to take him over their knees and spank him for smoking.

Even I had to remind myself he wasn't a little kid.

"Hello there, Fell. I hear you've been busy snooping around while I've been away."

"Your suitcase is at the desk," I said.

He didn't say thanks or anything else.

We started walking along together, toward the door that led from the courtyard back to the lobby. He had Plumsie tossed over his shoulder.

He said, "My mother said you wanted to ask me something."

"Your father said you wanted to go first."

"You go first."

"I'm having a lot of trouble with the idea the accident wasn't your fault, Little Jack."

"*Jack*," he corrected me, without any sign in his face that I'd say anything he didn't expect to hear. "That big old Caddy came right at us. It was like a suicide mission if you ask me. We couldn't have gotten out of the way if we'd wanted to."

"What about if you'd been sober and you wanted to?"

"Cork it, Fell. I wasn't that bad off."

"I remember you that day."

"I remember you, too. You finally decided you had a few minutes to spare Dib, and you thought he'd be so thrilled at the prospect, he'd drop everything."

"I should never have let Dib get in that car with you."

"What the hell were you in Dib's life? See you around, Kid, when I'm not busy being a kiss-ass Sevens! . . . Dib was the only friend I ever had."

"What about all those scruffy-looking characters you always had in your car?"

"I'm talking about having a friend. One who comes first."

I said, "He came first with me, too."

"Sevens came first with you. Dib told me that."

We were walking down the long hall toward the registration desk when he shot that zinger at me.

I didn't have an answer for it. It came like a punch to my guts.

"He should have just chucked you, but Sevens fascinated him. That's why he let you treat him like a doormat. He was curious about that club. That's the reason I wanted to get in touch with you. Let's sit over here a minute. This dummy's heavy."

He pointed to two captain's chairs. As we headed toward them, he got off a few remarks about Sevens that were more obscene than they were anything else. And naturally he said we were all faggots because it always comes down to that with Neanderthal types.

"If you were such a big friend of his, why didn't you get him in?" he asked.

"It doesn't work that way, and you know it."

"I don't pay any attention to Sevens. What I'm planning to do for Dib is something he'd want, not something I'd ever want."

"Well?" I looked at him while I waited for him to light another Camel from the old one. He was an insecure Neanderthal. He needed a prop when he talked.

"I want you to arrange to get him on The Seventh Step," he said.

On The Seventh Step outside Gardner Chapel there are gold footsteps with names on them. They're in memory of any Sevens who died while he was enrolled at school. A few were from World War I, more from World War II, when kids enlisted because they couldn't wait. . . . None from Korea or Vietnam. One was in a plane crash. One had had cancer.

In Sevens we joke about ending up on The Seventh Step, or seeing to it that someone else does. It's part of our slang.

I said, "Only Sevens get on that step."

Plumsie was stretched out at our feet, staring up at me. He had a little smile, like he was listening, amused.

Little Jack said, "So change the rule."

"The Sevens would never allow it, much less go to the expense for a nonmember."

"I'll pay for it."

"No, they won't let you do it!"

"I'm going to have some money soon. In a few hours, in fact."

"They're not going to make any exceptions. It doesn't matter if you have money."

"Don't say *they*. You're part of them."

"So I am. Thanks for reminding me."

"Gardner didn't use to take girls. Now they are. Things can change."

"Some things can, but this is a waste of time."

"I'm selling the dummy. The damn thing gives me nightmares."

"Maybe it's not the dummy; maybe it's your conscience."

The atmosphere in the place was getting to me, I think. I could swear Plumsie was laughing, that his chest was moving and his lips were stretching wider.

"Get off my case! I told you what happened. It's your *own* conscience bugging *you*, Fell!"

"I have a date," I said. "Forget The Seventh Step."

"I'm getting good money for this block of wood. I'm getting a couple thou. . . . Tell that to The Sevens."

Either Fen was taking him or they were both stupid. It wasn't my business. I wouldn't mind being around the day Little Jack found out he could have gotten a lot more thou than a couple, but that was that.

I didn't really have any more business with Little Jack. I realized that, finally. What was I going to do, hit someone who looked twelve years old?

I said, "I'm going." I stood up. He did, too, stubbed his cigarette out in one of those silver sand buckets, and picked up Plumsie.

"Not a bad price for something I dragged out of a car wreck."

I looked to see his face. The expression was wise-guy smug.

He said, swaggering a little now, "Sure, I swiped the dummy. Lenny Last was dead."

"So you made up the story he asked you to take care of Plumsie."

"Yeah, I made it up. I had a right to the dummy, considering what he did to my best friend and my dad's car. If this wood chip here can pay for one of those gold footsteps, then it's worth it. I'm not going to take your no for an answer."

"Do what you want," I said.

"Thanks, I will," he said.

He was still keeping up with me. He wasn't finished.

"The guy that's buying him? Fen? He says the damn thing's cursed anyway. I've heard others say the same thing. . . . He says that might have caused the accident."

"Then why's he buying him?"

"He's from Vietnam. He's from a culture that doesn't believe in our myths. He says the dummy he's got doesn't like her clothes." He guffawed, and looked up at me for my reaction.

I couldn't give him anything. I shrugged and said, "That's the way they talk."

"He wants the dummy right away because he's got a job tonight, so I'm going to take the money and run."

We were in front of the registration desk.

"You're John Fell?" the fellow named Toledo asked me.

I nodded, and he pushed a piece of paper across the desk, and said I was to call that number.

It was Keats'.

I'd probably need a room somewhere that night. I knew what the price of a room on the ocean was in summer, even in a place like Kingdom By The Sea. There'd be no lobster dinner at Gosman's unless I took myself down to the beach and konked out under the stars.

I told Toledo to give Little Jack the bag, and I left him without saying any more.

I escaped into a phone booth across the way.

Keats answered and began wailing that the cook had quit and her folks were having sixteen people for late supper after theater that night.

"I can't go anywhere, Fell," she said. "I have to help Mummy somehow. Don't ask me how."

"What was the cook planning to do?"

"We're up to our necks in shrimp. That's all I know. I'd say come here, but I wouldn't even have time to talk to you."

I was watching Little Jack come toward the phone booth carrying a suitcase.

Keats said, "Did you see Little Jack?"

He was carrying *my* suitcase.

"Keats," I said, "you gave the bellperson here *my* suitcase. You've got the one with all the dummy's stuff."

"I wondered if you'd shrunk," she said, laughing. "I peeked inside and saw this teensy tiny pair of jockey shorts." Then the wailing began again. "I could kill Cook! She ruined everything!"

"Keats," I said, "tell Mummy I do fantastic things with shrimp. When I worked at Plain and Fancy, shrimp was on the menu of most of our buffet dinners."

"That's right! *You* cook! That's right!"

"Tell her that if she doesn't mind having the cook spend the night in the room with the waterbed, the ocean view, and the private bath with the sauna, I'd be happy to do her party."

"Can you do it all by yourself, Fell?"

"No, not all by myself. You'll put on an apron and assist me."

Keats giggled.

8

THE MOUTH

Christmas 1962.

Over Sheep's Meadow and through the park to Grandmother's house we go.

"Do you really live here?" Lenny's question was answered for him by the doorman.

"Good evening, Mr. Nels. Miss Annette said to tell you she and Celeste went out for dinner."

The Fifth Avenue apartment that had once been Nels' grandparents' place was one full floor, the front windows facing the Central Park Zoo.

It was all dark wood and thick rugs, embroidered pillows on silk sofas, leather-bound books, and paintings in rich, gilded frames.

A butler named Lark had let them in and repeated the doorman's message. He'd been smirking as he did.

Nels said, "They're usually not even here for the holidays, but the *Seastar* decided to bring in outside entertainers this Christmas. . . . Lark hates it when they're home."

"Then you both live here?"

"The three of us live here: Annette, Celeste, and me."

"Wow, Nels! A whole floor to yourselves! What a way to live!"

"It would be if Celeste wasn't around. We even have room for more, but Celeste won't allow anyone else to live here. She doesn't care a fig for Father's wishes."

The hall they were walking down had walls adorned with old masters, each with its own light.

Nels continued. "My father'd tell Annette never to thank him for adopting her, but to remember it by adopting her own child one day. Do you think Celeste would ever let that happen?" He gave a snort.

He stopped in front of a door at the end of the hall. "Wait 'til you see this, Tra La."

It was a girl's room with everything in miniature. The canopied bed, dresser, desk, chair, and velvet-covered chaise longue. Tiny closets all the way around the room were open, exposing frilly little dresses on hangers, and elaborate shoe trees all filled with minuscule high heels.

There were several red wigs on stands.

The room was a mess, clothes strewn about, makeup left open atop a small vanity in the corner, various coats on the backs of chairs, and one white fur thrown to the floor.

"As you can see," said Nels, "Celeste isn't very neat."

Lenny was used to that kind of talk by then. He just let remarks about Celeste's personality and habits go by.

"A dressmaker does her wardrobe," said Nels. "If my sister's been invited someplace formal tonight, Celeste will be in a gown, complete with evening slippers, evening bag, real pearls, real diamonds, and probably the mink, since there's the ermine on the floor."

"I'm dying to meet her," Lenny said. "And your sister, too, of course."

"One of these days you will."

"Not this vacation? . . . I was counting on it."

"Not yet, Lenny. It isn't time yet."

Then he changed the subject. "You should see all the jewelry Celeste has! Laura would turn green with envy."

"You've got Laura all wrong. She doesn't care that much about all that."

"She cares, though. She *does* care about it, Lenny. You should have let me pay for that Seven of Diamonds for her Christmas present."

Lenny couldn't get it through Nels' head that he and Laura weren't even engaged yet, and that when the time came for something that expensive, Lenny'd want to pay for it himself. For Christmas, Lenny had barely been able to afford the gold 7 to go with the gold chain Nels had given her. In the winter there were fewer rentals of the white Cadillac.

"You have too much false pride, Tra La."

FELL DOWN/99

"Pride, maybe. But not false pride."

"I'd *loan* you the money, if that'd make you feel better."

"Laura would know where I got it."

"So what! The time to get her something beautiful is when she's young and beautiful. She'll be old and wrinkled when *you* can afford it, *if* you ever can." Nels laughed. "An actor spends a lot of time in the unemployment line."

"I'll take care of Laura."

"Someone like Laura ought to find trinkets from Cartier under her pillow at night and baubles from Tiffany in her coat pockets."

"I think I know her better, Nels."

"You haven't got any romance in you, Tra La. How sad for Laura."

Then suddenly he said, "Let's get out of here!"

"We just got here," Lenny said.

Lenny kept mumbling protests all the while they went back down the hall, got their coats from Lark, and found themselves in the polished wood and brass of the little elevator, descending.

Hailing a cab, Lenny said he'd have liked to see the rest of the apartment, at least, and Nels snarled, "I feel like getting plastered!"

Then he pounded Lenny's back good-naturedly and flashed him a smile.

"Let's go, Lenny. I know a place they don't check ID's."

They headed downtown in a taxi. Soon they were

standing at the bar in Joe's Rathskeller, holding schooners of suds, singing "God Rest Ye Merry, Gentlemen" and "Roll Me Over."

After Nels spotted a redhead who was not many inches over five foot, he told Lenny he was going to concentrate on her. "Toodle-oo, Tra La. Leave if you want."

"I probably will." He was starting to feel his drinks.

"Give my love to Laura when you call her later."

"Okay."

"We must make a plan, Tra La. It's time to start making a plan."

He was standing on tiptoe, cupping his mouth with his hand, funneling what he had to say into Lenny's ear.

"A plan for what?" Lenny could tell Nels' beers had hit him hard. He only said "Toodle-oo" when he was bombed. It was part of Celeste's sign-off, and his sister ended her letters that way.

Lenny had trained himself not to get angry when Nels tried to tell him how to treat Laura, as he had back at his apartment.

He knew it wasn't easy for Nels, suspected Nels was half in love with Laura.

"We have to plan the kidnapping," Nels said. "Start thinking about where we'll dump our victim, what ransom we'll demand, that sort of thing."

"Oh, are we kidnapping somebody?"

"Shhhh. Don't talk too loud."

"Who are we kidnapping?" Lenny was amused at

the idea that Nels was so plastered. Nels never lost control, never rambled. But here he was back on the old kidnapping theme.

"We're not kidnapping anyone right away," he said.

"When are we going to do it?"

"A little under a year from now. We'll be on a trip."

"I think you're traveling in outer space right now."

"No, I'm not. But I am planning our trip."

"And we're going to kidnap someone on it?"

"Yes, Tra La."

"Who's the lucky fella?"

"It's not a fella," said Nels. "It's Celeste."

9

Adieu was on Dune Road, at the top of a hill over-looking Seaville and the Atlantic Ocean.

I expected Eaton, their butler, to answer the door, but he wasn't on duty.

Keats' father did the honors instead.

"Hello, John." He was in a dark suit, always.

"How do you do, sir?"

Gras, the two-ton dachshund, was growling at my pants cuffs, while Lawrence Keating eyed the suitcase I was carrying, his mouth turned down.

"So!" he said. "I'm told you're here to rescue the supper party."

"I think I can," I said modestly. I knew I could.

"We want to pay you too, John."

"Oh, no, sir. I'm doing this as a favor to Keats."

"She tells me you do this sort of thing profession-ally," said Himself, sticking a hand down his pocket and rattling his change. "I never designed a house for anyone free of charge."

I felt like saying, Try it, you'll like it.

But he wasn't the type.

I said, "I like to cook."

"I liked what I did too, John, but I expected recom-pense."

Mrs. Keating came rushing out then like a little bird running down a lawn. She was thin and tiny, always very tan and quick to smile. She had on a long, red dress.

"Hello, dear. My my, you didn't waste any time getting here."

I was still carrying my suitcase, but I stuck out my left hand and we shook.

"Speaking of time," Mr. Keating said, "if we're going to the Stewarts' before theater, we'd best get started."

"Sweetheart, I have to show John the kitchen and see what he can make of all that shrimp."

"Do you have bread and salad greens?" I asked her as we went down the hall.

"Yes, plenty of both. And luscious tomatoes!"

"Then don't worry . . . Dessert?"

"We have cookies. We have peaches."

"Peaches, good! I'll do peaches with bourbon. You have bourbon?"

"Of course. . . . The help have the afternoon off, but

they'll be on duty again at seven. This is awfully nice of you, John."

"Everyone calls me Fell."

"I know, but I can't call someone by his last name," she said. "And at ten o'clock, for entertainment, we're having one of those ventriloquists from the convention."

"Was that Keats' idea?"

"No, we didn't even think our daughter would be here this weekend. Someone from the club told me about this young Vietnamese. He's performed at The White House!"

"Fen," I said. Fen trying out Plumsie!

"Yes, that's his name, dear. I wish there was someone to put your suitcase up in the guest room."

"I'll do that, Mother," said Keats, rounding a corner wearing an apron and a maid's cap.

"Darling, what *have* you got on? I thought you were cooking the shrimp."

"It's cooked," she said. "All Fell has to do is shell it." She took my bag and blew me a kiss.

"Did Mr. Keating speak to you about payment, John?"

"He did, ma'am. And I told him I didn't want any."

"Oh, dear, dear, dear. He'd be more impressed if you took something, you know."

"I'm not trying to impress him," I said.

"Anymore," she said.

▣

After I shelled the shrimp, I made layers of shrimp,

onion, lemon, and parsley in a casserole.

Keats was assisting me by sitting on a stool waiting to show me something she said was a surprise.

I'd asked her to let me get things under control first.

"Shall I preheat the oven, Fell?"

"This isn't going in the oven," I said. I added more lemon and parsley, also tabasco. Dripped some olive oil over that, and topped it with bay leaves. "This will marinate for four hours, then it's ready to serve."

"Men are sexy when they cook."

"So are women," I said.

"I think I've lost it, Fell."

"Lost what?"

"My sexual feelings and my sex appeal."

I was cutting little red new potatoes in half, dunking them in olive oil, ready to pop into the oven in a few hours.

"You're still sexy," I said.

"Don't be flippant. I'm discussing something sincerely with you, or trying to."

"I'm sorry," I said. "I'm trying to get dinner ready for sixteen people."

"Eighteen counting Daddy and Mummy. . . . I really mean it, Fell. I'm bored with sex. The whole idea of it bores me. It even repels me."

I sighed.

"You don't want to hear about it, is that it?" she said.

"No, that isn't it. . . . I feel the same way sometimes."

"You do?"

"I just can't get interested in anyone."

"Ever again?"

"I hope it isn't permanent."

"I have a sneaking suspicion I'll never again be really interested *that way* in anyone. I'll probably marry someone I like but I hate going to bed with. It'll be awful, too, because you don't like to turn down someone you really like, and yet there's no way you can stand sex night after night when you're not horny yourself."

I recognized a true Keats tirade gaining momentum. Her theme hadn't changed much. It always centered on her own worthlessness, how she would never amount to anything, blah blah, blah blah. It was the kind of anxiety rich girls suffered from before they jumped into their sports cars and broke the speed limit hurrying somewhere wonderful to shop.

My own mother, who wasn't rich, got on the subway and headed to Macy's when she was upset over anything too.

Keats and my mother just didn't get upset over the same kind of thing.

"Where is the corn?" I asked.

"Are you listening to me? . . . It's right by your feet, under the table."

"Keats, let's not worry about ourselves tonight. We're doing good things here. We're saving your folks' supper party. Later we'll see Fen and the famous Plumsie!"

There were about fifty ears of corn in a box.

"I've had this feeling for a year," Keats continued. "I haven't been horny for a year! I don't even have good dreams anymore. I dream in clichés. I'm flying or I'm falling or I'm shopping in my underwear."

Thank God for the now-and-then nights that brought me dreams of Delia.

Keats said, "Corn is a terrible idea for old people at a party! It gets caught up in their crowns."

"Your mom and dad are only in their forties."

"Only? Who wants to be almost fifty, Fell?"

"At least when you're fifty, this man you've married who you like but can't stand in bed won't be after you night after night."

"There's that," she said.

"Help me husk the corn," I said.

"No, I've got a surprise, remember?"

"It's going to keep you from husking corn?"

"From doing anything but reading to you."

"I thought you were going to assist me?"

"I put the maid's apron and cap on. I was all set to. Then I thought I'd better lie down and put my feet up for a few minutes, just to rest . . . and I opened something to read. It's a journal I found in the suitcase with the dummy's things. It was under a shelf in his makeup kit."

"I wonder if Little Jack knows about it."

"I bet he doesn't. The Horners didn't mention it."

"It must have been Lenny Last's."

"It's more like a story, Fell."

"It's more like an excuse not to husk corn."

"A story about Lenny Last *and* Nels Plummer."

I made a grab for it. "Let me see that thing!"

"No. I want to read it to you."

"Who wrote it? Is there a name inside?"

"No name. It sounds like some third party telling about Lenny Last meeting Nels Plummer. It starts at Gardner school, or on the bus going there. I've been skipping around a lot. The handwriting's horrible."

"Read it," I said.

"Please."

"Please."

Outside on a chaise, Gras was sleeping on his back, all four paws and long dachshund nose sticking straight up.

Beyond him were a dazzling emerald-green pool, rosebushes, a croquet game waiting on the lawn for someone to play it, and, just over the dunes, the Atlantic Ocean lapping at the beach.

I promised myself before the summer was over I'd get Mom and Jazzy out to Coney Island or Riis Park for a picnic.

Keats began to read.

"'Ruby is my birthstone,' Laura said. "'Someday I want a real ruby. . . . Do they cost . . .'"

"Wait a minute," I said. "Who's Laura?"

I remembered Mrs. Violet saying how Lenny Last had carried on about her name being Laura, that he'd told her he'd known someone named that, and she was a shrink now.

"Just listen," Keats said. "They're at one of The Sevens' Sunday tea dances: Lenny, this Laura, and Nelson Plummer himself! I'll start at the beginning of the entry.

"It took The Sevens to turn the worst part of any weekend into the best."

9

THE MOUTH

It took The Sevens to turn the worst part of any week-end into the best.

The Sevens' Sunday tea dance got under way around four in the afternoon. It went until nine or ten, when the boarding-school girls had to catch the last trains and buses out of Cottersville.

The basement of Sevens House was transformed into a grotto. The girls were given blue caps with 3+4 in white letters on the peaks, or 6+1, or 2+5.

Stevie Wonder and The Beach Boys came through the speakers, Bobby Vinton and The Four Seasons, and a new group called The Beatles, singing "Love Me Do."

It was at the last Sevens' Sunday tea, the day before graduation, when Nels got Lenny and Laura to go out

FELL DOWN/111

back, to the white Cadillac, for a surprise.

Lenny had worked hard to keep it running well and looking even better. He rented it out for proms and Saturday-night trips to Philadelphia. In winter it had been protected by a shed Lenny'd made for it in the Sevens parking lot.

After they piled into it, Nels said, "Guess what Celeste gave me for graduation. . . . Psychoanalysis!"

"That'll cost a fortune!" Laura said.

"She's the moneymaker of the family," said Nels.

The late-afternoon sun was starting down in a pink sky. The campus smelled of honeysuckle and roses.

"I thought you were supposed to pay for your own analysis or it wouldn't work," said Lenny.

"You are," Laura said.

"Psychoanalysis is just the care of the id by the odd," said Nels.

"Oh, Gawd, I've got to write that down!" Laura laughed.

"That's all it is," said Nels. "The care of the id by the odd."

"We heard you the first time," Lenny said.

Laura said, "Lenny? What's bugging you?"

"Tra La doesn't have my golden tongue," said Nels. "It's hard to be average when your best buddy is superior."

□

But both boys knew what was bugging Lenny.

It was Nels' crazy idea to kidnap Celeste and ask for a $50,000 ransom.

112/FELL DOWN

Lenny could have the money. The money didn't matter to Nels. What he wanted was to destroy Celeste.

He said what he wanted was to have his sister back.

"How do you know she won't just get another dummy?"

"She won't. There isn't another Celeste—and she'd never settle for less. No. Without her, she'll retire."

"Is that what you want? You want her home with you?"

"Home. Back. Yes."

"Does she have that much money, Nels?"

"Don't worry about my sister. She's still got every cent she inherited from my father, and she's my heir, too. Fifty thousand is peanuts to Annette!"

"But what if she won't pay it?"

"She will."

"She could go to the police!"

"The ransom note will warn her that going to the police means the end of Celeste."

"But Nels, how are you going to—"

Nels would cut him off. "Let *me* take care of the details, Lenny. I'll come to you when I'm ready."

▢

Both boys knew how much $50,000 would mean to Lenny at that point in his life.

He could marry Laura and put her through medical school, the one thing she wanted most.

Otherwise she'd be shipped off to Oral Roberts' new university. Since she was a pastor's daughter as well as an A student, she'd been offered a scholarship there.

Lenny would be stuck in New York City, trying to get

a job doing anything, waiting for the lucky break that'd head him toward Broadway. Some actors never got there.

Nels was planning to take some courses at Columbia, nothing strenuous, and live at home. He'd be around to remind Lenny he'd had his chance once and he'd let it slip through his fingers. Too bad, hmmm?

The scheme made Lenny nervous, angry, hopeful, afraid, and not too sure Nels' love for his older sister was all that brotherly. . . . Was that any business of Lenny's?

◻

Lenny had crawled into the backseat of the Cadillac while Laura sat in front with Nels. Even though Nels never drove a car, he liked to be in the driver's seat.

Nels snapped on the radio, and the Drifters came through it singing "Ruby Baby."

"Ruby is my birthstone," said Laura. "Someday I want a real ruby. . . . Do they cost much, Nels?"

Notice who she asked.

She knew Lenny wouldn't have a clue.

"They're not as expensive as diamonds," said Nels. "You should have both."

Laura laughed. "Hear that, Lenny? When your rich Aunt Martha dies, I want a ruby and a diamond!"

Months ago, Lenny had started mentioning an Aunt Martha, saying he hoped she'd live through her heart bypass, that the money she'd leave him would never be worth the loss.

Nels had told him he couldn't just wake up one morning $50,000 richer without some explanation to Laura.

114/FELL DOWN

Next to Lenny on the backseat were three boxes, wrapped in white paper and tied with gold ribbons.

"After tomorrow," said Nels, "we have to stop wearing things with Sevens on them. School's out."

Laura covered the gold 7 around her neck protectively. "I'll never stop wearing this. It'll always remind me of the first time I ever came to The Hill."

"Laura, take off your cap," Nels said. "Tra La? Would you pass around those packages on the backseat?"

"I hope these aren't graduation presents," Laura said. "I don't have anything for you, Nels."

"You're not rich and I am."

Lenny was taking Laura to her school prom and the party after, in a Philadelphia hotel suite. He had saved enough to pay for the satin gown she had wanted and her father had told her was "the devil's creation."

Lenny was renting a tux for himself and buying a white-orchid corsage for Laura.

Already his expenses were close to $500.

When he had told Nels that, Nels had answered, "Chickenfeed for someone like Laura, Tra La."

Any chance he got, Nels had begun reminding Lenny how much $50,000 could change his life. And hers, too. Mostly hers, he'd admitted. Laura had more dreams.

"Besides," he'd added, "the best schools are in the East. I'd have my two best buddies close by. That way I don't have to go to college myself. I'll get my education through you guys, vicariously."

The three of them unwrapped the packages.

Inside each was a white cap and a white sweatshirt.

Written across them in red: THE TRIP TO NOWHERE.

There were tickets inside the caps, and announcements of the sailing, on the *Seastar*, five months away.

Passengers leave from New York at midnight on November 21st, and travel with no sight of land and no destination until the morning of November 24th, when they find themselves back in New York City.

Eat, drink, and be mysterious.

Be prepared to attend a costume ball on the last night out. Take advantage of our thirty-foot lap pool with a swim-up bar. . . . For golf buffs a nine-hole putting green, and on bridge deck a six-wicket croquet court.

Ask the ship's masseuse to relax you and the ship's astrologer to tell you what's ahead for you. Play backgammon with the ship's champion, and learn the latest dance steps with the ship's instructor.

Dancing nightly in the ballroom to Peter Porter's orchestra.

In the lounge, CELESTE—with Annette, of course.

Each deluxe stateroom has a private veranda.

   —The Seastar, Martin Stirman, Captain.

"It's something to really look forward to!" Laura said. "Now I don't feel so badly about going away with Daddy this summer!"

In July she was bound for Africa, part of a missionary

conference her father'd arranged for her to attend.

Reverend Delacourt had his eye on Lenny. He was on his knees nightly praying against him, and in his study a good part of every day plotting for ways to get Laura out of reach.

"We'll have one bang-up reunion!" said Nels. He glanced back at Lenny and gave him a wink. "And you'll get to meet Celeste, at last! . . . Celeste, my sister, and Captain Stir-Crazy. Of course we'll be in deluxe staterooms. Tra La and me in one and you in the other, Laura: *muy* proper."

After Lenny'd put Laura on the bus back to Philadelphia, he went to Nels' suite in Sevens House.

"I don't know if I can do this to your sister," he said.

"You don't have to *do* very much at all, Tra La."

"But it's major *tsuris* for her," he said, suddenly remembering his mother's Yiddish for woe. The Yiddish always came back when anything troubled Lenny deeply. "Why should I do it to her?"

"*I'm* doing it to her. I'm doing it *for* her. . . . Tra La, she's playing some tacky lounge on a ship with all these guys tossing back drinks, you can imagine the crapola she takes!"

He was packing.

He was piling his Brooks Brothers suits on the bed, and his Turnbull & Asser shirts on the dresser.

Two large steamer trunks were open on the floor, waiting to receive his wardrobe.

Lenny sat down in the big, soft leather Eames chair Nels had ordered for himself and was now leaving behind for the next occupant of his suite in Sevens.

"You're the only person I've ever trusted, Lenny."

"I trust you, too. But this is different."

"Yes. It's different. A once-in-a-lifetime opportunity, Tra La . . . and it'll be the easiest fifty thousand dollars you'll make."

"*If* we can pull it off."

"Oh, we will."

"Not many kidnappers get away with it."

"But we're dummynapping, Tra La," said Nels. "And our little victim can't tell on us or die. She'll just disappear into the deep blue sea. Deep-sixed."

Lenny stretched his long legs out in front of him and stared at his old, scuffed Thom McAn loafers.

He shook a Kent out of a pack and lit it. He'd been smoking cigarettes ever since January, when Nels had finally convinced him he was serious about this thing.

"Your sister must like being on the *Seastar*, though. Maybe she doesn't think she takes crapola."

"I purposely never introduced you to Annette," said Nels. "I didn't want you to get fond of her, or you'd never want to do this. . . . So put her out of your mind. My sister is too complicated. Our relationship is too unusual to explain."

Lenny grinned finally. "You'll have to shell out for your own analysis after it's done, Nels."

"No. Because then I won't need it. Celeste has always been my only problem."

10

I made Keats go back and start the journal from the beginning. I'd long since finished the corn, and I was sitting opposite her on a stool, fascinated.

When the front-door chimes rang, I wished we could just ignore them so she could keep reading. But Gras flew off the chaise outside and came running in, barking nonstop, dachshund style.

"Whoever that is, tell him we don't want any," said Keats.

I headed down the long hall as Gras raced ahead of me.

Fen spoke first, introducing himself, starting to say something about wanting to see where he'd be working that night.

"I like to check the acoustics, the space, and—"

Then Plum spoke up. "Oh, shut up! Just zip it!" and

perched on Fen's arm like a big bird, he turned to face me. "And who are you?"

"John Fell," I said. "I brought your clothes with me from Pennsylvania."

"You can take those clothes and shove—"

"Plum! Is that any way to talk to someone who did you a favor?"

"Then tell him Finders keepers, losers weepers."

"Finders keepers," said Fen. "We don't want anything from Plum's past. You'll see why tonight."

10
THE MOUTH

"Tick tock tickers! Where's my Snickers? Tick tock tickers! Where's my Snickers?"

Celeste's voice was drowned out by the shriek of the *Seastar*'s whistle, and the moan from its horn.

Midnight. Time to sail off into the dark, friends.

"Tick tock tickers! Where's my Snickers?" A white gardenia was pinned to her red wig.

Annette smiled at Lenny and Laura. "No matter how many times we've sailed, it still makes Celeste a little nervous to leave land, and she needs her Snickers."

"At your service," said Nels, putting one of the candy bars into the dummy's coat pocket.

"No, no, Big Guy. Put it in my evening purse!"

Annette said, "Put it in my evening purse, *please!*"

"He knows where he can put it!"

"Celeste!" Annette said.

She looked embarrassed for the dummy and she said to the others, "I have to apologize for Celeste. Don't judge her by this performance."

"No, please don't," the dummy agreed. "This performance is a little wooden, wouldn't you say?"

The five of them were on deck. Behind them an oompah band had just finished playing "76 Trombones."

There was a full moon. The big ship pulled out while visitors from bon-voyage parties waved and blew kisses.

Laura spotted her brother, Carl, in the crowd and called out to him, "Don't tell Daddy!"

Lenny tried not to stare at Celeste. Nels had told him not to show any interest in ventriloquism, so he would not be suspect when the dummy was taken.

Lenny tried hard not to stare at Annette, too. She was not at all what he'd expected. Lenny wouldn't describe her as "fat." Big, yes, nearly six foot. Overweight and quite handsome, dark eyed, swarthy, short black hair she slicked back. She was clearly no relation to Nels. With her Amazon build, she looked like Wonder Woman in a Dior gown and high-heeled slippers.

Around her neck was a purple silk scarf, and a small nosegay of violets was pinned to her ankle-length mink coat.

The flowers were from Captain Stirman, she'd explained. She'd bought herself the mink. She'd bought one for Celeste, too. Of course. What did you think?

Lenny was racking his brain for an excuse for what

he was going to help Nels do to her. The minks would do it! He'd never liked women who wore furs. What kind of a person lets little animals be killed so she can parade around in their skins? His mother'd taught him to think about that. She could always turn their inability to afford luxuries into something noble.

A ventriloquist's dummy in mink! *Oy!* His mother would have held her head in pain. *Oy vay iz mir!*

Annette and Celeste were having late supper in Captain Stirman's cabin shortly. Lenny had met the Captain only briefly, but he had recognized the possessive gestures: the hand at her elbow, on her back, up on her shoulder . . . the eyes waiting for hers, the mouth soft, the face besotted.

The next morning Lenny put his greatcoat over his pajamas and stepped out on the private veranda.

It was nine thirty. In four hours he would be in the service room behind the dining hall. After lunch Annette performed. At the finish she came behind the curtains to set Celeste down in a chair.

Then, as Annette took a bow alone, received a bouquet from the Captain, and spoke briefly to her fans, Lenny would pounce.

He would grab Celeste, put her into a garment bag, and go into the ship's health spa, a door away.

Through the spa to the other entrance, out the door, and up a flight of stairs to this cabin.

The garment bag would be hung in the closet until nightfall.

FELL DOWN/123

Then bricks would be added to its bottom, and Lenny would step out on the veranda again.

So long, Celeste.

▣

There were contingency plans, of course.

But that was the main one. Quick and simple.

▣

Lenny went back inside the cabin, his cheeks wet with sea spray.

Nels said, "You want to hear the ransom note?"

He was sitting on his bed in white silk pajamas, shivering from the blast of cold air Lenny'd just sent his way. He was sipping coffee and finishing toast.

Lenny said, "I ought to check on Laura."

"Don't you know by now she likes to sleep in?"

Lenny felt like punching him.

It was nerves, not Nels, he reasoned with himself. Nels was always telling him what Laura liked, what Laura was like. Lenny and Laura had even joked about it together, calling Nels "The Big L.A." secretly. The Big Laura Authority.

"Listen, Tra La!" Nels said.

The note read as follows:

Celeste will be all right if you follow directions.
If you don't, Celeste will be destroyed.

1. See to it that your butler has $50,000 in cash, in a pillowcase, in $100 bills.
2. He drops it from your back bathroom window

into the alley at 11:00 A.M. Sunday morning.

3. He answers the phone at 11:15 A.M. He will be told where Celeste is on the Seastar.

4. He will call the Seastar *no later than 11:20 A.M. to tell Miss Plummer where Celeste is.*

ANY ATTEMPT TO MARK BILLS, TRAP RETRIEVER, SEARCH SHIP, OR IN ANY WAY HINDER THIS OPERATION WILL BE MET BY DESTRUCTION OF DUMMY.

DO NOT FOOL WITH US AND YOU WILL NOT BE SORRY.

FOLLOW DIRECTIONS FAITHFULLY.

"I hope we can trust Lark," said Lenny.

"Lark loves me like a son," Nels said, "and he doesn't have to do very much. Annette will call our lawyer and the cash will be sent over to Lark. He keeps a thousand for himself—that makes him more than an accessory—and then he claims he lowered the rest from the window. . . . He says he waited for the call saying where Celeste was and it never came."

"Won't they want to know where Celeste is *before* they hand over the fifty thousand dollars?"

"If it was a kid, they might. But they'll figure no one would gain anything by destroying a dummy . . . and a dummy can't tell on the dummynapper. They'll go along with it. After you hang Celeste up and leave here, you slip the ransom note under Annette's door, right?"

"Right. Then I come looking for you."

"And Lenny, if you're going to miss lunch because

you feel slightly seasick, start acting sick."

"I plan to."

"But before you do . . ." Nels reached under the pillow on his bed and took out a small blue box. He was grinning.

"This isn't for you, Tra La. It's for Laura. It's a premature wedding gift."

"I haven't even proposed to her."

"You're going to tell her your aunt died, right?"

"Yeah."

"Tonight. Right?"

"Shouldn't we wait until we have the cash in hand?"

"Tonight is the time," said Nels. "And this is from Uncle Nels."

He handed the box to Lenny.

"Remember I said she should have diamonds *and* a ruby?"

Inside the Tiffany box was a small Seven of Diamonds.

Where the horizontal bar joined the vertical, there was a ruby instead of another diamond.

"The ruby's for her birthstone, remember?" Nels said. "I can't wait to see her face!"

He gestured for Lenny to return it, and while Lenny was saying whatever it was he said at that point (Lenny could never remember), Nels put it in the inside pocket of his tweed sports coat, next to him on the bed.

"For now it stays with me," said Nels. "I'm keeping it with me until we surprise her with it! I figure a good time is after dinner, when the dancing's started. That's the time to pop the question."

Lenny did remember he asked Nels, "Do you want to do it for me?"

But Nels only laughed.

Nels didn't notice the anger in Lenny's tone.

11

As soon as she saw Fen, Keats decided she'd be the one to show him where he was performing that night.

I thought she'd let out a squeal or a holler when he introduced Plum to her, but she behaved as though nothing could faze her.

When she finally got around to seeing how I was coming in the kitchen, she could hardly talk.

"What's the matter?" I asked her.

She leaned against the counter, holding her head with one hand, breathing in deeply, then letting it out.

"Are you all right, Keats?"

"I will be."

"Where's Fen?"

"I made him put the dummy in the car. Plum's so mean, Fell. Was he mean to you?"

"Plum is a stick of wood. *Fen* told me to take the suitcase full of clothes and shove it."

"That's not Fen at all. Fen would never say that. That's Plum."

"Never mind."

"Fen says Plum won't need his old things at all."

"Did you tell him about the journal?"

"No."

"Don't."

"Is he out in the garden? Can you see him?"

I could. Gras at his heels, Gras' tail wagging acceptance as they strolled down a stone walk near the rosebeds.

"He's there. . . . Did you ask him why he wanted to buy Plum so badly?"

"I didn't ask him anything about the dummy. I hardly said anything. . . . Fell, my heart is coming through my blouse."

"*Why?*"

"Because of him."

"*Him?*" I looked again. He was very tall and very skinny. Silky, straight black hair like Gras', and the mustache . . . "What's so great about him?"

"I don't know."

"I mean he's probably a nice guy, but—"

"Never mind, Fell. Something's already started."

"Well, before something is almost over, try to find out how he heard about Plum, and why he wanted to own him."

"I think he's Japanese. He looks rich, doesn't he?

And he's driving a new Porsche."

"He's Vietnamese," I said.

"That's right. Mummy said he was Vietnamese. Oh Gawd, Fell, I don't know anything about Vietnam, even where it is exactly." She grabbed her head then. "And my hair!"

"It's fine."

"I've got to fix it! I've got to put on some lipstick. . . . Fell? I have another surprise besides the journal. It's upstairs in the VCR in the guest room."

"*I Love Las Vegas?*"

"Right."

"Thanks, Keats." But she was gone.

▣

Later, I watched them walk along together. Keats had changed to white shorts and a purple T-shirt. I could remember when she'd teased me about having purple eyes, and how one whiff of Obsession (which the downstairs reeked of suddenly) could make me go weak.

They stood down by the fountain in the rose garden for a while. He was all in white, except for a light-blue shirt and a dark blue-and-white-polka dot tie.

Everything he had on fit him so well, he had to have a Mr. Lopez in his life.

I started fixing the peaches, glancing out at them from time to time.

Their eyes never left each other's face, and every time I looked, they were grinning together or laughing aloud.

I began to feel tired . . . not just of what I was doing, but of what I wasn't doing, feeling, having in my life.

I cleaned up after myself, took the journal with me, and headed up the back stairs to the guest room.

I remembered the times I used to sneak down those stairs, nights I wasn't supposed to see Keats, on orders from her old man.

I flopped down on the bed and it gurgled. I turned on the VCR, and *I Love Las Vegas* began with that old early-sixties music sound when Tina Turner was still with Ike, and my mom was in high school learning all the dance steps from the Mashed Potato to the Watusi.

She could still remember most of them.

All you'd have to say is Mom? Do the Funky Chicken.

Mom? Do the Hully Gully.

◙

The windows in the guest room were very tall and wide, so you could lie on the bed and look out at the ocean. Its color was early-evening green; the sky was still pale blue.

I kept thinking about Jazzy, for some reason . . . about maybe taking her someplace for fun . . . so she could get away, say she'd been someplace that summer when she got back to school.

I didn't feel like fast-forwarding to Celeste. I just let the movie play, and I picked up the journal.

Elvis was singing "She Thinks I Still Care."

The handwriting was tiny and not easy to read, but I finally found the place where Keats had stopped.

If you're ever curious to see Annette and Celeste in action, catch the movie I Love Las Vegas.

11

THE MOUTH

If you're ever curious to see Annette and Celeste in action, catch the movie *I Love Las Vegas*.

Elvis is in it, so it's still around, mostly on late-night TV.

It's all there:

Dr. Fraudulent telling Annette that psychoanalysis is just the care of the id by the odd.

Annette asking Celeste if she'd like to join her secret sorority and Celeste saying she hoped it wouldn't interfere with her membership in the Book-of-the-Month Club.

Celeste announcing that Annette was on a seafood diet. She sees food and eats it.

And of course, her trademark:

CELESTE: For sunburn or windburn, I turn to my Swinburne.

ANNETTE: Oh, no, Celeste.

CELESTE: Mr. Swinburne, you know me so.

ANNETTE: Honey, we don't want to hear those gloomy poems again. We want to be cheerful. There are young lovers in the audience.

CELESTE: Hello, young lovers! . . ."I wish we were dead together today/Lost sight of—"

On and on. (You'd think Nels'd never had an original thought!)

Ending with . . . the old song Annette used to sing to Nels when he was little.

"Seeing Nelly Home."

And Celeste would interrupt and say . . .

🔲

"Who *wants* him home? He is a horse's *derriere*!"

The audience aboard the *Seastar* loved it.

Some of them who'd seen the act before had Snickers bars with them for Celeste.

Laura had to laugh despite herself. She whispered to Nels, "Does it make you furious when Celeste says that?"

"I could kill her," Nels smiled back.

🔲

It was one twenty-six, close to her finale.

Lenny was ready.

He was trying not to think about Nels or Laura while he waited for Celeste to be placed in the chair.

He was trying not to think about marriage, too.

When it had been a kind of faraway dream, it had seemed idyllic, but now that Nels was forcing it to happen way ahead of time, Lenny had cold feet.

He imagined all the *tsuris* he'd get from his mother because Laura wasn't Jewish.

And he'd have to face Reverend Delacourt's threats of vengeance, if not in this life then in the next.

Nels loved to orchestrate other people's lives, didn't he? Not other people's, either . . . just theirs: Laura's and Lenny's. He'd probably arrange to be along on their honeymoon.

And if Nels had his way, and Lenny did propose right away, what would Laura remember about the night?

Six diamonds and a ruby.

Still . . . $50,000 was such an unbelievable amount to come Lenny's way when he was only eighteen.

If he'd never met Nels, he'd probably be in some chorus line, or waiting tables as he'd been doing for months, hoping for a break . . . even a walk-on in an off-Broadway play.

Laura would probably have drifted away from him.

◻

Suddenly Lenny heard the *Seastar* audience singing:
I was see-ing Nel-ly ho-oh-ome . . .
I was see-ing Nel-ly—
The next thing Lenny knew, the dummy was in the chair.

◻

Everything went without a hitch.
Lenny hung up the garment bag with Celeste inside

and shut the closet door. He sat on the bed and lit a Kent.

He wouldn't have minded taking the dummy out to look at her closely, but he'd promised Nels he would not do one thing that was not in their game plan.

Maybe later, before she was deep-sixed, he could admire the handiwork that had gone into creating her.

He sat there smoking, just beginning to feel the thrill of what was going to be possible now.

He put out the cigarette, walked across to the mirror, and watched his reflection give him a smile and a wink.

He'd pulled it off. No small thanks to Nels, and to the anger he'd felt toward Nels when he was back in the service room waiting to grab Celeste. That had helped defuse the fear.

His face glowed. He could have everything now. Let Nels give her the stupid Seven of Diamonds!

He gave his hair a swipe with the comb, then had second thoughts: mussed it, stopped smiling, made his eyes seem sad. After all, when he caught up with Laura and Nels, he was supposed to be still a little seasick.

Lenny squared his shoulders and set off for the next step: the ransom note he'd leave under Annette's stateroom door.

She lived one deck above, near the Captain's quarters.

Lenny went up there and in one quick motion bent down and gave the envelope a push.

When he stood up straight and started toward the

stairs, he saw the Captain.

The Captain wasn't supposed to be there. Nels said the Captain never missed one of Annette's performances.

The Captain was coming out of his door with another *Seastar* officer.

From the looks on their faces, there was something wrong.

Part of the contingency plan was for Lenny to ask a silly question if he was seen someplace where he seemed out of place.

Make a point of it. If you were guilty of anything, you wouldn't.

So Lenny said, "Oh, Captain, is the Jacuzzi nearby?"

The Captain looked at him.

There was something very, very wrong.

"What?" Lenny asked, because he had never seen a man just let tears roll down his cheeks.

"President Kennedy's been shot in Dallas," he said.

The other officer said, "He's dead."

12

I was stretched out on the waterbed, holding the phone on my stomach, waiting for *I Love Las Vegas* to rewind.

"Of all the missing people, Nels Plummer's the one I remember best," Mom was saying, "because he disappeared the day the President was killed."

"What do you remember about him?"

"That he was from the food-chain Plummers. They're very rich, Johnny. I remember wondering why his sister had a job on a boat, when they had all that money."

"Do you remember that he went to Gardner and that he was a Sevens?"

"*Really?* That wouldn't have meant anything to me back then. So he was in your fancy club? Well, that figures."

Mom would never believe you didn't have to have money or pull or something special to be a Sevens. Since I couldn't tell her how you became one, I'd never convince her that wasn't it.

Now there was a new threat to the Sevens' secret. Keats had stumbled upon it in the journal. Even though she swore on her eyesight and her ability to feel emotion that she would never, *never* speak of it again, to me or to anyone else, I'm not so sure I would have sworn on those two essentials that she could be trusted.

The moon was rising over the ocean. The sun had set on any dinner plans I might have worked out with Keats.

Fen's blue Porsche was still in the driveway. No sign of them in the garden, but Gras was on the grass destroying a rawhide chew stick, which meant someone wanted him out of the way.

Mom was still talking about Nels Plummer. "I remember one theory was that he fell overboard upchucking. There was talk of all the drinking on that ship once the news was announced."

I still hadn't finished the journal, although I'd been trying hard to read it at the same time I watched *I Love Las Vegas*.

Thoughts of Jazzy'd kept intruding. I was thinking of what a lousy summer she was probably having.

"It's funny that you called right now," said Mom. "I've always thought we had ESP. Has Jazzy been on your mind?"

"I was thinking tonight that I ought to take her

someplace like Jones Beach or Fire Island, before summer's over."

"She couldn't wait. She's taken off by herself."

"What do you mean?"

"What I said. She's been missing two hours. Then you call up and ask me about a missing person. . . . Maybe she's at Aunt Clara's, up on the roof over there. They've got it planted. Clara maybe thinks I know Jazzy's with her."

"Sure. Where else would she be?"

"Bernard's walking over there now to see, and if she's not there, then we call the police."

"Bernard?"

"Mr. Lopez," said Mom.

"She'll be there," I said, "don't you think?"

"I don't think," Mom said. "It's wasted effort when it comes to your kids. I just react."

"Yeah," I said. "That's what I do, too."

"You, you don't know," said Mom. "You take off when anything gets you. You don't react. You take off."

"Do you want me to come home?"

"You're out there now. She's just at Aunt Clara's."

"She's there," I agreed.

"She'll be all right," Mom said. "Don't worry."

"Okay. I won't," I said.

"I'm glad you called, Johnny."

"Me too," I said. "I'll check with you later."

I looked at my watch. It was twenty past eight. Where was a five-year-old at twenty past eight in the evening if she wasn't at her aunt's?

I supposed Mr. Lopez would take care of it.

He was practically family, wasn't he?

Dear Lord, I hoped he wasn't. . . . There was something about Mr. Lopez I was never going to like—maybe the fact that most times I'd talked to him he had pins in his mouth.

There'd be this little hole in his lips words would come out of, and there'd be three or four pins.

That's how I remembered him.

The house was quiet except for the sound of music. It wasn't the Von Trapp family trudging down the Alps with Julie Andrews leading them in "Do-Re-Mi"—more like an old Madonna album, more like "Like a Prayer."

I supposed Keats was playing things for Fen. They were probably sitting on that great, soft, white couch in the living room with the French doors opening onto the garden.

No doubt in a little while Bernard would arrive back at our place with Jazzy in tow, and they'd put her to bed, then sit around in front of the TV the way they did, drinking homemade wine and eating Fritos.

To each his own, hmmm?

At such times I often found myself on the verge of trying to imagine what Delia was doing, who she was doing it with, and where. Rome? Hong Kong? Paris?

Then very quickly, before the stinging behind my eyes turned into salt water, I refocused my thinking.

I turned to something far away from me and my experience.

I turned on the little Tensor lamp and picked up the black leather book.

Of course, the only one on the Seastar *not upset about Kennedy was Nels.*

12

THE MOUTH

Of course, the only one on the *Seastar* not upset about Kennedy was Nels.

He refused the Captain's invitation for all passengers to assemble in Main Dining for prayers. Many were settled in there, watching the large TV flash the latest news bulletins from Dallas and Washington. Laura was among them.

Captain Stirman had announced that the *Seastar* was heading back to port. The ship would arrive in New York harbor at midnight. Two days ahead of schedule.

"This screws up everything, Tra La!" Nels complained in their cabin. "I've got to think! Go stay with Laura."

"Do you think your sister's read the ransom note already?"

"Has to have! I can't stop it now. When she was taking her solo bow? Someone opened the door and shouted, *'Kennedy's been shot!'* People started crying, screaming—Annette didn't get out of the room for about twenty minutes. That's when I should have moved: found you, put Celeste back, and gotten the note from Annette's stateroom. *Why* didn't I think faster? This is such lousy luck, Tra La!"

"We can't pull this off now, Nels."

Nels was pacing, hitting his fist with his palm.

He said to Lenny, "I need to make new arrangements, that's all. We'll smuggle Celeste out somehow."

"I don't feel up to this, Nels."

"What's the matter with you?"

"The President's dead, Nels!"

"Don't pull any crap on me, Tra La!"

"Don't you know what's going on aboard this ship? Everyone's in a daze."

"That could work *for* us."

"Let's just give her back the dummy, Nels, and forget it. It's all different now."

"No way. We've set things in motion. Lark is prepared and we are. We just have to rearrange the schedule, push it up. I'll figure it out."

"Won't the banks close down?"

"Not yet, and I bet my sister's already been on the phone and arranged to get the money."

"We can't count on anything running normally, even your sister, Nels. Laura can't even talk."

Nels opened his jacket and patted the bulge in the

inside pocket. "She'll have plenty to say when she sees this tonight."

"No, Nels. Everything's changed now."

"They'll still have dinner and dancing."

"No one's going to want to dance."

"You'll see. The show must go on. Their show must, and so must ours. Celeste is about five hours away from her watery grave . . . just as soon as it turns dark."

Lenny said, "Did Jackie Kennedy get shot, too?"

"Damn you, Tra La, pay attention to *us*!"

"We're stopped. At least for now."

"We're not stopped. You know, I didn't plan this for myself, Lenny."

"Didn't you?"

"This is all for you and Laura."

"For Laura, anyway."

"I don't have time for this. Go and be with Laura."

"Don't do us any more favors, Nels."

He stopped pacing and faced Lenny. "What does that mean?"

"I'm going to quit while I'm ahead."

"Don't be a fool!"

"The President's shot and you're pacing around planning how to do your sister in!"

"You're a mush head, Tra La. You've got mashed potatoes for brains!"

His eyes were narrowed and his hands were balled to fists. "You don't deserve Laura!"

"I thought that was it, all along. You wish you had her, Nels, but you don't and you won't and you can't!"

Lenny laughed in his face, even though his stomach was turning over.

Lenny was almost crying then. His voice sounded younger and sillier and shrill. "You've always wanted what was mine, from my childhood stories to my Handy act to my girl. You can't make it on your own! That's why you want your sister home, and it's why you want Laura and me in New York."

"I don't deserve this from you, Tra La." Nels' voice was very calm.

For a moment Lenny thought Nels was going to talk to him, make things okay again somehow, take back the ugliness between them.

Instead he socked Lenny, hard.

Lenny lit into him as though all he'd ever been waiting for was an excuse to beat up Nels.

No holds barred.

When Nels finally fell to the floor, there was blood trickling from his mouth. His right eye was already swelling to a slit.

Lenny looked down at him, amazed at what he'd done.

He leaned over, put his hand out, ready to pull Nels up.

"I'm sorry, Nels."

But Nels shook his head and pushed Lenny's hand away as he propped himself up on one elbow.

"Get the hell out of my sight," Nels said quietly.

◻

When Nels didn't join them all evening, Lenny figured he was angry, and probably resigned to the fact there was no way they could follow through on their plan. He hoped Nels was with his sister, as Laura thought he might be.

Laura was frightened by the assassination. She had put in a ship-to-shore call to her brother, although Lenny had tried to discourage it. Twice she sent Lenny back to the stateroom to find Nels, but he wasn't there. The garment bag was. Still.

Laura kept saying she bet Nels was taking it hard.

Lenny finally snapped back. "Nels doesn't give a damn about Jack Kennedy or anybody but Nels! Don't you know that?"

"You've never really liked Nels," Laura said. "He loves you and you just use him."

"He uses us, too."

"How?"

"I'm not going to analyze it now."

"You can't. Because he doesn't."

Lenny decided not to continue the argument. They made a halfhearted effort to eat dinner. No one in the dining room was finishing. Few were even talking.

"I didn't mean anything I said a while ago," Laura finally ventured. "I just feel very insecure."

"Same here," said Lenny.

"When we get to New York, I'm going on home with my brother, Lenny. Do you mind?"

Lenny lied and said he didn't. He knew he was losing her.

He wished that suddenly Nels would come around

the corner with just the right thing to say, and the perfect thing for the three of them to do . . . because Nels could always do that.

If anyone was looking for Celeste, Lenny wasn't aware of it. Nearly everyone was glued to the television. Some were praying; a small group was singing songs like "God Bless America." The bar was doing a good business.

⊡

After the *Seastar* docked, Reverend Delacourt, with Carl, came aboard to take Laura back to Philadelphia.

Neither one would speak to Lenny, or believe that Laura had occupied a separate cabin.

"Well, good-bye," Laura said.

Lenny had to turn away. His eyes were full.

⊡

When Lenny went to get his things, there was still no sign of Nels. His luggage was there. And Celeste was still hanging in the closet, in the garment bag.

Lenny slung it over his shoulder and carried it off the ship with his own luggage.

He didn't know why he did it.

People, that day, were not thinking about why they did what they did.

Lenny took a cab to his mother's. All through the early-morning hours, Celeste sat in a chair across the room from them while they watched replays of Johnson taking the oath of office, and of Jackie Kennedy coming home in her blood-stained pink suit with her husband's coffin.

148/FELL DOWN

13

No, Plum would not need his old clothes.

Fen sat in a flood of light, on a stool in the garden of Adieu. Star, in black satin and pearls, was on one knee.

And on the other?

Celeste, in white satin . . . looking exactly as she had in *I Love Las Vegas.*

The only difference was around her neck.

The Seven of Diamonds . . . and where the horizontal bar joined the vertical, there was a single ruby.

◻

But how could it be?

In the journal Nels Plummer had it in his jacket

pocket the day he disappeared.

The show began:

CELESTE: Tick tock tickers! Where's my Snickers?

STAR: I ate them, dear. It seems I was always coming across them in the pockets of the tacky clothes I had to wear.

CELESTE: Even my hand-me-downs are too classy for you, love. You don't understand class or Swinburne, or—

STAR: *My* favorite poet is Billy Idol.

CELESTE: That will never do, love, if you're to perform with *moi*. You have to change.

STAR: The way *you* changed? Folks, she changed from a male into a female. She's one of your transsexuals.

CELESTE: It's time for a songfest!

STAR: To drown out the truth, Plumsie?

CELESTE: *I was see-ing Nel-ly ho-oh-ome, I was*—
Join in everyone!

"And now what do you think of poor old Plum?" a voice asked.

I turned to face Guy Lamb. He had on a cowboy hat and boots, the same bolo tie with the turquoise stone, the black belt with the silver buckle. At that party he stood out like a Froot Loop in a china bowl filled with bonbons.

He didn't wait for an answer to his question.

He said, "At last I know what became of Celeste. She was turned into Plumsie. I should have figured that out long ago. There aren't that many McElroy figures still performing." He popped a shrimp into his mouth as a uniformed maid passed with a tray. "Very tasty!" he said. He wiped his mouth with a paper napkin that said Adieu.

I figured it'd be *adieu* to him as soon as one of the Keatings spotted him. He'd obviously crashed the party. Not another soul there looked like him; no one looked as if they even knew someone like him.

"How did you get here?" I asked him.

"I was just going to ask you the same question."

I told him how I had. He said he'd come there to sell Fen an alligator figure case Fen'd wanted to buy. When he couldn't find Fen all afternoon, he found out Fen had a date at Adieu. "I'm leaving early tomorrow morning. I'm glad it worked out this way. I wouldn't have missed this for anything."

"What do you think? Did Fen know he was buying Celeste when he bought Plum?" I decided to get as many questions in as possible, before he got the boot. I knew the Keatings. They wouldn't tolerate a gate crasher.

I didn't have time to tell him anything about the journal. Where I'd left off, Lenny had taken Celeste from the boat the night of Kennedy's assassination.

Guy Lamb shrugged. "I don't know what to think. Celeste was way before Fen's time. She was from the early sixties . . . and Lenny Last came along with Plumsie near the end of the sixties. But Fen knows her pretty good, I'd say. That's Celeste, if I ever heard her. That's how she looks, too, and that's how she dresses."

He shook his head sadly. "Maybe that lady who owned Celeste sold her to Lenny and then Lenny did the worst thing."

"What's that?"

"Changed her sex. You don't do that. It's very bad luck. . . . No wonder Lenny went downhill."

The Keatings' guests were joining in singing "Seeing Nelly Home."

We had to shout to hear each other.

I asked him if he remembered that something had happened to Annette Plummer's brother.

"Yes," he said. "He was a missing person. You think that's why she sold Celeste? Too broken up to perform after?"

I shook my head as though I didn't have a clue.

He said, "What's your connection in all this, Fell?"

"None."

"It doesn't sound that way." He grabbed another shrimp from another maid's tray.

It was around eleven o'clock, with a cool ocean breeze and a full moon overhead.

I could see Keats way down in front, her chair as close as she could get to Fen.

After the song, Celeste started doing Dr. Fraudulent.

I was as amazed as Guy Lamb, who hit his head with his fist and said, "Golly darn! She's the real thing!"

"What about the necklace?" I asked him. "That's new, isn't it?"

"It's a fake. Star was wearing that same seven yesterday by the pool. I asked Fen if it was insured. He said it was just a copy. . . . So that surprises me. Celeste would never have worn a fake in the old days."

"Did Fen say who had the original?"

"I didn't ask him. You sound like a claims adjuster, Fell."

Just at that moment I saw Mrs. Keating heading our way.

I figured Guy Lamb was going to be pointed toward the garden gate.

It was me Mrs. Keating wanted.

"I'm sorry to tell you this, John," she said. "Your mother called. Your sister is missing. The police are looking for her."

▣

Whatever Eaton's official title was (Caretaker? Butler? Estate Manager?), he became my chauffeur that night.

While I waited for him down in the driveway, I stood beside Fen's Porsche.

When my mother's in a strange house, she likes to take a peek in the bathroom cabinet. She says you can tell a lot about someone by seeing the bottles and tubes lined up on the shelves.

The closest I could come to discovering anything about this fellow was by reaching into his car for a look in his glove compartment.

Eaton caught me at it.

He said in his sourest tone, "Of course you know that's not the car we're going in."

He was carrying my bag over to the black Lincoln, after giving me one of his looks. I used to suffer them when I was dating Keats.

"I don't know why Mr. Keating is being so generous to you," Eaton said. "Perhaps he's just glad to get rid of you."

I kept my big mouth shut.

I didn't feel like a skirmish with Eaton. It never pays to get the driver ruffled when you're going a long distance.

We were about two and a half hours from Brooklyn.

And I was too worried about Jazzy.

I wasn't so rattled that I didn't notice that the bag Eaton was putting into the back with me was not mine. I was about to make off with the little clothes and the journal again, but this time it suited me just fine.

On my excursion into Fen's glove compartment I'd discovered his address and his last name on his automobile registration and his driver's license.

I had an excuse now to pay a call there, pretending that I thought Fen would want what was inside the suitcase.

You see, Fen lived on Fifth Avenue.

His last name was Plummer.

13
THE MOUTH

Lenny'd fallen asleep in front of the TV. It'd been on all night. He didn't even hear his mother leave for her job at Macy's next morning. He woke up in time to see Lee Harvey Oswald shot dead.

Then the phone rang.

"I'm glad I got a hold of you, Leonard. This is Captain Stirman."

Stir-Crazy . . . probably hunting down Celeste.

Lenny had to turn down the sound to hear him. He wondered if he should tell him Oswald had been killed.

"Is Nels with you, Leonard?"

"No. Didn't he go home?"

"We haven't seen him. His sister and I are very, very

concerned. When did you last see him?"

"Just after Celeste and Annette performed. Around two."

He could have sworn Celeste was smiling at him from the rocking chair. "He wanted me to be sure Laura was okay, so I went down to Main Dining to be with her."

"I saw him about an hour later. Did you and Nels have a fight, Leonard?"

"No. Why?"

"Someone had worked him over. He *said* a kidnapper did it, and Celeste *is* missing. There's even a ransom note. What do you know about it, Leonard?"

"Nothing! I'm sitting here watching what's going on in Dallas. Did you know someone just shot the guy who shot Kennedy?"

Lenny needed time to think. Was this a trick of Nels'? Was Nels trying to pin something on Lenny?

Stirman said, "I'm taking care of my own before I start worrying about Kennedy and the rest of it. . . . Nels told me he tried to stop a masked man from taking Celeste."

"I told you. I know nothing about it."

"Nels said he thought Celeste was thrown into the sea in all the assassination confusion."

"It's news to me."

"Would your girlfriend know anything about it?"

"Of course not!"

"May I talk to her, please?"

"She went home with her family."

Lenny gave him the number. Lenny hadn't spoken to Laura since they'd said good-bye aboard the *Seastar*. He had the feeling it was good-bye forever. He had the feeling he would not fight for her left to his own devices. But Nels would make him do it. Nels would never let her go.

On television they were replaying the most recent shooting. Lee Harvey Oswald was grimacing, holding his stomach in pain.

Suddenly the world seemed to have gone mad.

Lenny imagined that Celeste was winking at him.

"Nels will show up soon enough." Lenny told the Captain what he had been telling himself over and over. Nels was either hiding somewhere to punish Lenny or he was working on the kidnapping. Lenny doubted Nels was doing that, or he'd be frantic about Celeste's whereabouts. He'd have called Lenny long ago.

The Captain began asking him about girls in Nels' life, saying there had to be some.

Lenny said, "Why? He was always bashful."

"Did you ever know him to buy jewelry for a girl-friend?" the Captain asked.

"No. Did you?" It was a strange question. Had Nels shown him the Seven of Diamonds for some reason?

The Captain said, "I don't know him as well as you do. Would he buy jewelry for his sister?"

"I doubt that. Why?" Somehow the Captain *must* have seen the gift for Laura. Next Lenny imagined the Seven around Laura's neck, the three of them together again, this all forgotten.

He could still see Nels' bloody face, one eye closing.

He could still hear Nels telling Lenny, I don't deserve this from you, Tra La.

That was right. Nels hadn't deserved it.

◻

The Captain dropped the subject of the jewelry.

Lenny had crossed the room and picked up Celeste. He had never seen a figure so beautifully made. The head was molded in plastic wood; the eyelids and retractable lips were fashioned from leather, and skillfully grafted onto the head.

There was a plate behind her ears, which opened to a spaghetti network that made her moves and expressions possible. There were levers inside that looked like typewriter keys.

The Captain said, "When Nels gets in touch with you, tell him we're calling the police. I only waited because I didn't believe that whole story he told me, and because our problems seem so minuscule compared to what the country's suffering. But now we have to take steps. Celeste is very much a part of our concern, too. She is extremely valuable. I'm not speaking now just of sentimental value. She is unique."

Yes . . . Lenny could see that. He was fondling Celeste's headstick. . . . Valuable . . . complex.

"Take this number down, Leonard. It's my private phone. If you hear one word from Nels, call me. I'll make it worth your while. . . . Dear God, where *is* he?"

◻

It was a question that would obsess Leonard Tralastski

long after he'd submitted to the police inquiry . . . long after he'd become Lenny Last.

He would never stop wondering about Nels.

Sober, he would think of all the possible accidents Nels could have had. (Ill from the punches to his gut, Nels had leaned too far over the ship's railing.) He would toy with the idea Nels had amnesia from the blows to his head. (Nels had just walked off the ship in a daze.)

Drunk, he would suspect everyone of murdering Nels, including himself. Could he have blacked it out? Hadn't he, deep down, wished Nels dead sometimes?

Nels would haunt him forever.

◻

But that Saturday afternoon, on the 23rd of November, it was Celeste he became fascinated and obsessed by.

He hung up the phone and bounced her on his knee like a proud father.

"Well, well, well, well," said he, "how's the little lady doing?"

He typed inside her head until she tilted a little to the right. She grinned into his eyes.

"What makes you think I'm a lady, Mac?"

"What makes you think I'm Mac? I'm Lenny."

"How do you do? You can call me Plumsie."

"I thought your name was Celeste."

"My *old* name was. I'm Plumsie now."

"How do you do?"

"Get me out of this drag, will you?"

Lenny's fingers typed some more and the figure put

its hands on its hips and looked back at Lenny and rolled its eyes.

"Wipe off my lipstick, would you, Big Guy? And lend me a snappy necktie."

That night Lenny threw the red wig down the incinerator in the hall of the apartment building.

He'd get him a new wig when the weekend was over. It was Lenny's idea to rig Plumsie up so that even Nels would be fooled when he saw him.

14

Back in Brooklyn, home sweet home.

"You must promise me never to do that again."

"I was only downstairs," said Jazzy. "Make Mom give Georgette back to me."

"Mom's trying to teach you something. You know how upset you feel now without your doll? That's how she felt."

"She didn't even know I was gone for a long time. She was down the hall at Bernard's."

"Mr. Lopez to you. Not Bernard," I said.

"Mr. Stinkmouth to me! I want my doll back and I want *him* dead!"

"I'll get Georgette for you, but don't run away any-more. Not even down to the laundry room. Okay?"

"*You* run away, Johnny. You've done it twice times. From school once, and once from the restaurant."

"Two times, not twice times. I'm not going to run away anymore," I said. "Neither are you, kiddo!"

I went down the hall and knocked on Mom's door. It was half open. The light from the television was still on.

"Are you awake, Mom?"

"She can't have Georgette. Not until tomorrow."

"Mom, it's already tomorrow. It's three A.M. She can't sleep without Georgette."

"Tough, Johnny! Do you know what it's been like around here tonight? No, of course you don't. You were off in The Hamptons with your rich girlfriend."

"May I come in a second?"

"Don't talk. This is almost the end."

How many times had she seen Ingrid Bergman walk away from Humphrey Bogart at the end of *Casablanca*?

I sat on the edge of her bed.

It was my second or third time. It was one of the few movies my dad had liked watching on TV. We used to tease him that it was only because he bore a slight resemblance to Claude Raines, the actor who played the dapper police chief.

I spotted Georgette leaning against a Kleenex box on the shelf behind Mom.

Jazzy used to dress her as a ragged, poor person, then change her into fancy costumes: ball gowns, silk dresses with sequins, queen's robes.

I waited until the music's swell and the credits.

Then I picked up Georgette. She had on jodhpurs and a riding jacket.

"My kingdom for a horse," I said.

Mom sighed. "All right, take it to her."

"He's the one upsetting her," I said. "Bernard."

"Would you kids be happy if I'd set fire to myself the way widows used to do in India?"

"You know how Jazzy felt about Daddy. . . . If there was ever a daddy's girl—"

"Talk to her, Johnny."

"I did. I will some more."

"I shouldn't pass this information on to you, since you think Mr. Lopez is only fit to darn and stitch, but we were talking after Jazzy got home and we could think straight again. Mr. Lopez happens to be fascinated by the Bermuda Triangle. He knows all about your Nels Plummer."

"How does Mr. Lopez think Nels Plummer got anywhere near the Bermuda Triangle?" I said in the same tone Eaton had used on me.

"Never mind. You're too superior to talk to, I can see that."

"Mom, the *Seastar* wasn't anywhere near that part of the Atlantic where all the planes and ships disappeared!"

"Bernard knows that. But Nelson Plummer disappeared in 1963, and in 1963 a tanker with its entire crew disappeared in the Bermuda Triangle, and so did two Air Force tankers. Bernard buys anything to do with it, and he has a book across the hall about missing people. Your Nels Plummer is in it."

I said, "Thanks, Mom."

"Bernard's not your dad, but he's not what you're making him out to be."

"I know. But Jazzy and I think even Mr. Rogers wouldn't be good enough for you."

"You're right about that."

□

When I dropped Georgette on Jazzy's bed, she said, "Have you got a doll, Johnny? Where'd you get all the neat clothes?"

"I told you," I said. "They belong to a ventriloquist's dummy."

"I wasn't listening to all that stuff about ventrilquims. I was missing Georgette."

She was hugging the doll, settling down under the covers. I put a sweater of Plumsie's back inside next to the journal.

Then I changed my mind and picked the journal up to take out to the Hide-a-Bed where I sleep in the living room. There was a lot I hadn't read, and a lot I never would. But if I could make out the handwriting, I was game for one last read . . . the few pages at the very end.

"Do you promise to hang around from now on?" I asked Jazzy.

"Do you?"

"I'll be around until I go back to school," I said.

"Okay, me too," she said.

14
THE MOUTH

And now, of course, it's time for me.

I'm not really a writer, you know, even though more and more I have had to rescue the act with my own material.

Sample:

If Leonard feels a little wheezy,
(Asthma does that) . . . well, it's easy,
For then the act becomes old Plum's,
And in the darkness someone comes,
Someone wet and someone hissing,
"Would you leave me down there? Missing?"

Oh, it would get him very, very crabby, that would.
"Leave Nels out of it! . . . You're no writer, Plum!"
I never reminded him that it's me writing this thing

so it looks like a story—and why? So Tra La De Da doesn't have to face that it's his very own autobiography.

He likes to distance himself from himself, you see. From himself, from everybody. That began way back when he said toodle-oo to Laura. He gave her up, or she gave him up. We'll never know, since he didn't call her again. I take a little credit for that—Old Plum is on the selfish side, doesn't like to share . . . doesn't even like the *word* unless you're talking about a piece of cake.

Maybe I'm not a writer, but who cares? I don't even read writers. I read nothing.

I'm a boob-tube geek.

Ask Tra La. When he's out drinking and gambling away our hard-earned money, I sit and watch the big picture.

When he drags his behind home, broke, he sits beside me watching, too, and he says, "What a pair we are, old buddy."

I know how to get him.

Say I, "Who do you mean, you and Nels?"

Once he cried.

He said, "When are you going to leave Nels out of it?"

"What if he comes back and he finds out we left him out of it? He won't like that one bit, will he?"

But back to me.

I like what's hot!

Writing in this journal is not hot, so I told him *ce soir* (that's Spanish, dear hearts. It means this evening)—I told him no more scribble scribble, Leonard.

Your life history is over, say I.

Finito . . . (that's French for finished).

Do you get it *YET*, *amicos and amicas*? (That's Russian for friends.) Ha! Ha! Get the picture? . . . I lie for enjoyment. Others golf, shoot pool, jog, and you know what, but I like prevaricating. . . . Doesn't that sound filthy?

Say I, "No more scribble scribble, Tra La."

Say I, "What your future holds now can never be recorded, and you know it, Tra La. Nothing about this can be put down in writing."

(There were times when he'd cry out, "Don't call me Tra La!" but he doesn't fight me anymore.)

Say I, "Lovely to be back in Cottersville, is it not?"

Says he, "It's not."

Say I, "You're at Sevens House again, eh? And you're on another of your little trips down Memory Lane, hmmm?"

Pause.

Say I, "You may answer, Tra La."

"Knock it off, Plum. This is different. I've never killed anyone."

"That you remember, Tra La. Your mind is shot. I doubt sincerely (don't you love me using that word?) that you'll remember anything about this visit to your old alma mater either . . . but it will get us out of debt, Tra La."

He has no reaction. Sits there like a lump.

Say I, "They couldn't have made it any easier for you, and what a cute little gun they got you, Tra La."

FELL DOWN/167

Say I, "Revenge is sweet, too, isn't it? Particularly when The Sevens set it up. . . . Answer me, Tra La De Da."

Says he, "There's no such thing as The Sevens Revenge."

Because, you know, he was *taught* to say that. They teach them all to deny there's any such thing.

Say I, "At least they knew who'd welcome *any* kind of work, even dirty work."

Says he (speaking without permission—*tsk! tsk!*), "I didn't need to buy a rat for the job, either, since I have you."

Which is *why*, Ladies and Gentlemen, Boys and Girls, Fans and Foes, I refuse to leave this lovely old white Cadillac, even to go inside Sevens House for a minute.

Leave me out of it is my new motto, and I told Tra La I was parking my carcass in the car.

Where I will wait . . . and wait.

Old Plum is good at waiting.

And I like old cars.

Lately I have longings for old things . . . things like Snickers bars, which Tra La brings me.

Say I, "Thank you, Big Guy."

Makes him wheeze to hear me call him that.

Wheeze wheeze, Louise: His asthma is worse than ever now.

It's why I took over the act in the first place, you know.

Nobody wants to pay to hear someone gasping for air in the middle of a joke. Toodle-oo to boo-hoo-hoo.

Lately I have longings for old things.

Said I that?

Easter is in the air, that's why—Easter vacation.

Easter always reminds me of when I was Celeste.

I was known for my Easter hats.

Is that a song I feel coming on? . . . Oh, *In my Eas-ter bon-net . . . with blah blah blah upon it . . .* Who wrote that, pet, do you know?...A box of Snickers to the lady in the front row who answered Ozzy Osbourne.

We always have to credit the author, don't we?

Pictured here is Nels Plummer, 18, of New York City, scion of a wealthy food family, who vanished on board the luxury liner Seastar *in 1963.*

He was last seen in his cabin by the Captain at 3 P.M. on the afternoon Kennedy was shot in Dallas. The ship was nine hours north of New York.

Annette Plummer, the sister of the missing man, rules out suicide. The skipper of the 16,567-ton vessel states that the heir to a fortune could not have accidentally fallen from the ship, which was constantly in serene waters. "Those railings are four feet high, even on the private outdoor verandas. I defy anyone to fall off my ship, unless a person climbs up on a railing and jumps."

Investigators declare that leaves only one conclusion: murder.

—from *Still Missing* by George Tobias.

14

I had the feeling that Bernard Lopez had bought the Tobias book only to get me over to his apartment.

The book was so new, some of the pages were still stuck together. I think his interest in the Bermuda Triangle was zilch, too. He had nothing to say about it when I asked him.

This is what he wanted to say.

"Johnny, I'm no brain, but any problem you might have taken to your dad, feel free to come to me about. I'll do my humble best."

I felt like telling him to shove it, felt like saying I'll look you up when I want to know what's the best thread to use on a coat hem, or how to fit a hammer foot attachment to a sewing machine.

But I felt sorry for the guy. Did he *really* think my mother'd get serious with *him*? Or that he'd turn out to be just like a father to me and Jazzy?

He kept rubbing his long, skinny fingers together and whining that he hadn't had time to "pick up" because Jazzy'd run off.

His apartment looked like the back room of a tailor shop, one of those places where the guy watches TV while he works. He was watching a Sunday-morning news program, chain-smoking Benson & Hedges and sipping something he called coffee/I called rotgut.

I was glad to get out of there, even though it meant getting on a subway next. It was shaking from side to side, stinking of garbage and don't-say-it, rushing me under the East River and into Manhattan: God's country, next to Brooklyn . . . or was it anymore?

Now New York looked like some ex-lover whose beauty was still showing, even though she was homeless, and standing in the gutter with a needle in her arm. You wondered if it was too late for her to go back to what she used to be.

I'd called Annette Plummer, so she was expecting me.

15

I could hear the church bells ringing down the street at St. Patrick's, and over on Park at St. Bartholomew's.

Lark must have been sneaking up on eighty, a wizened, white-haired old man in a navy suit that had seen better days too. Going up to the third floor, Lark told me that he operated the elevator for the Plummers himself now that the building had gone self-service.

He said Captain Stirman was at church, but Miss Plummer only went on holidays, or when her son was home.

"I didn't know she had a child."

"She adopted this little boy, Fen, from Vietnam, right after her brother disappeared. You know about the brother?"

"Yes."

"Is this about him?"

"No. Not really."

"But Nels has something to do with why you're here?"

I nodded.

I was tempted to ask him if he'd ever received his $1000 from the ransom money for Celeste, but he looked so frail I couldn't.

He said, "There's a writer name of Tobias comes here every so often. Lark, he says, anything new? . . . What could be new after all these years, am I right?"

He was fishing.

"You're right," I said. "What could be new?"

As he let me into the apartment, he said, "She likes to talk about Mr. Nels, though, so don't worry about bringing up the subject. . . . And she's very happy this morning. Very, very happy. Fen found something for her we all thought was gone forever."

She looked very happy. All smiles as I came off the elevator directly into her apartment foyer.

"Come in," she said. "I just spoke with Fen."

"And he said he didn't want the clothes."

"No, we want them." She led me down a marble hall, carrying a cigarette in a long gold holder, continuing, "Fen said maybe our dressmaker can do something with those tiny suits and sweaters and shirts. Put lace on the cuffs or change the buttons to pretty little pearl ones. . . . Of course Celeste is such a snob she won't agree to wearing hand-me-downs, but the other one will."

She laughed. It was a strangely thin and lilting laugh for one so enormous. Her hair may have been as white as Lark's behind the Clairol, but it was raven black, slicked back in a wet look, her eyes a vivid green, the sort that watched yours to see what she could learn about you.

And she did like to talk about "Mr. Nels," particularly after I told her I was attending Gardner, and I was in Sevens. She said "Nelly" was crazy about that club.

She was drinking black coffee, letting me refill her cup from a silver pot. I was having orange juice, served by Lark in a long-stemmed glass.

On the coffee table was the photograph she'd hunted down to show me when I told her that the night before, I'd watched Fen work with Celeste on one arm and Star on the other.

In the photograph there was a curly-haired young boy in one of those old-fashioned-looking sailor suits with short pants and knee socks, and a big bow tie in the front.

While I studied the picture, she talked.

"Celeste won't tolerate Star in the act for long. She's always been the whole show, except for when she was younger. Then I'd make her share with Nelly. See him there on the right?"

He was sitting on one of her knees, and the dummy was on the other. Celeste had on a matching sailor suit, except hers had a skirt instead of pants.

Annette Plummer grinned down at the photo. "Those were happy days. Little Nelly'd pretend he was like Celeste. I taught him a whole routine to go with hers. He got it in his little head it was better to be made of wood than flesh and blood. . . . He wanted a room like Celeste's, too, with everything scaled down to size, but Daddy said no. Daddy said, He's going to grow up thinking he needs you to talk or smile or walk or think!"

In the picture, little Nels was leaning forward to get a look past Annette to Celeste.

The two females were both smiling at the camera, but Nelly was staring at the dummy, as though he was checking to see what she was up to.

"Was Fen good?" Annette Plummer asked me.

"Very!"

"I taught him everything I know, and of course Celeste is everything I know. . . . Even when I thought I'd never see her again, I taught Fen her routines. From the time he was just a little tyke. . . . He was five when I adopted him. I was keeping a promise to my father to adopt a child."

"You and the Captain?"

"No. Fen is mine alone. The Captain and I aren't married. One day he'll talk me into it, I suppose, but for now we just live together."

She smiled at me, lighting a cigarette for herself. She seemed in a mood to talk: not really lonely, but not sorry that I'd dropped by, either.

"This is a big place," she said. "Room enough for

everyone." She waved her hand toward the large room with all its antique furnishings and works of art. Thick rugs. Old vases. Flowers everywhere. Through the long windows, I could see the treetops across the street at the Central Park Zoo.

She blew out a few smoke rings, as though she was clearly satisfied with herself that Sunday morning in July.

I decided to jump in.

I said, "Celeste was wearing a Seven of Diamonds around her neck."

"Of course, you'd know that. Yes. It's a copy. The original is in my safe. I'm very surprised Celeste wore the copy. Star would, of course, but *Celeste*?"

I didn't bat an eye.

I said, "I've never seen one quite like that. Who gave it to you?"

"Nelly, of course," she said. "It was his last gift to me. He told the Captain he'd ordered it especially for me."

She shook her head. "Here he was in pain from being beaten up. You know my brother's case, don't you?"

"Yes, I know it."

"I guess everybody does, no matter what age. Nelly's become like Judge Crater or James Hoffa. Legendary."

"Yes, you could say that."

"The person who took Celeste beat him up. May

have gone back and killed him later, but the Captain saw him in the meanwhile. Nelly wanted to be sure that I got the Seven of Diamonds immediately. He told the Captain it might cheer me up, so he wasn't going to wait until journey's end to give it to me. He knew how I loved John Kennedy. I was the only Democrat in the family."

I remembered the journal: the description of Nels with the jeweler's box inside his sports coat, just before the fight with Lenny.

"It's the first one I've ever seen with a ruby," I said.

"Nelly didn't get a chance to tell me about that, but I guessed," said Annette Plummer. "A piece of bright-red color in a row of diamonds. It could only stand for Celeste in my life, with her red wig. It was terribly original, which surprised me because Nelly wasn't all that original. He always copied from other people. Daddy said I'd done that to him by making him play dummy all the time. It wasn't like him to think symbolically: He was so direct. But what else could the ruby stand for?"

For Laura Delacourt's birthstone, I thought.

Annette Plummer said, "Of course Nelly loved drama! He loved doing dramatic things, and he could afford to. What Nelly wanted, Nelly got. I'm afraid Daddy led him to believe there were no limits for him."

She stopped smiling and looked off toward a vase of long-stemmed white roses, shaking her head.

"Maybe that's why I went off to sea," she said in a sudden, merry voice, as though she was mocking herself. "I ran off to sea like some young boy. I skipped college, said toodle-oo, and took off. For years I wrote Nelly every day. Much as I adored him, I had to get away."

"Was he controlling, was that it?"

"Not controlling, really. No. He was beginning to turn into me. It's hard to explain, but if Nelly truly admired you, he became you. It was as though you'd absorbed him. He was there but he was you. It was rather frightening. Whatever it was, he had no way of his own. . . . It's hard to explain, Fell."

Thanks to the journal, it wasn't hard to understand, though. Leonard Tralastski had made the same complaint about Nels.

Or Plum had . . . if you wanted to believe they weren't one and the same.

"Celeste never trusted him, you know," she said.

I had no response to that remark, and she went on.

"Nelly knew it, of course. A part of me used to think Nelly'd destroyed Celeste himself, then changed his identity. But how could Nelly just walk out on his inheritance? He could never have afforded himself. He brought several new suits a month . . . and shirts, shoes. He was a world-class shopper."

"My mother's one of those."

"The Captain isn't chopped liver when it comes to shopping, either—only what *he* likes you can't bring home on the bus in bags. You steer home the things he likes."

She lighted yet another cigarette, in a mood to talk.

"A few years ago the Captain learned there was this broken-down ventriloquist who played the casinos and sang 'Seeing Nelly Home' in his act. The Captain began to suspect Celeste had not been thrown overboard after all. When he found out that Lenny Last was Nelly's old school pal, he was sure. But he didn't want to say anything to me. I had almost put the whole tragic affair behind me. And how could he ever prove it?"

I had an idea I knew why the Captain didn't want to say anything.

He didn't want her coming face to face with Lenny Last and finding out what the ruby really stood for, and whose necklace it was to be before the Captain took it.

Took it and then did what to Nels Plummer?

Had the Captain sent Plummer to a watery grave, just as Nels had wanted to do to Celeste?

Had the Captain found Nels injured from the fight with Lenny, and then finished the job himself?

But why?

Annette Plummer had more coffee.

Then she began to answer the questions I would have liked to ask her . . . the very ones I was sitting across from her asking myself.

She said, "The Captain always felt threatened by Nelly. My brother and I were like some kind of night-club act when we were together: playing straight man for each other, doing one-liners that cracked each other up—oh, you know how it is when you're very, very *simpatico* with someone. . . . The Captain was jealous of Nelly. Celeste spotted it almost immediately, and as the Captain would come toward us, she'd say, 'Here comes jelly belly, jelly of Nelly belly, jelly of Nelly.' I'd have to hush her."

Maybe all vents were space cadets when it came to their dummies. So far I hadn't met one who wasn't.

I said, "When did *you* find out that Celeste wasn't destroyed—that she was really Plumsie?"

She looked insulted suddenly, and her eyes narrowed. "Celeste was never Plumsie! Plumsie tried to take her over, yes, but Celeste was too strong for him!"

I said, "Sorry."

Her face softened. "I am, too, Fell. I shouldn't be cross when you only came here to do us a favor . . . And here I've been blabbing away selfishly about myself and Nelly and Celeste. Forgive me!"

"I'm having a good time."

"I think I miss having a young man to talk to. Fen's such a good listener."

"Please go right on with the story," I said.

Another smoke ring. She admired it for a moment, and then got back on the subject. "As soon as Lenny Last was dead, the Captain told me his suspicion. They were more than suspicions by then. He'd actually had Fen sneak off to a performance of Plumsie's out in Las Vegas. Both of them vowed to get her back for me. And for Fen, as well. . . . Fen knows Celeste's entire act, but he can't make it work with Star. She's clearly inferior."

"Not a McElroy," I said, straight-faced.

"Far from it!" said Annette Plummer, looking pleased that I understood.

She said, "You see, the Captain would like to have Celeste back on the *Seastar*. Fen would like living on shipboard, too, I think. And I am happiest at sea. We could all four be together. It'll be enormous fun!" Her face was radiant then. "Celeste will *love* hearing what we've planned for her!"

She rose finally and said it was so very nice to meet someone from her brother's school . . . and club.

"Although," she said, "There are some very ominous things about The Sevens, aren't there? Some kind of Sevens Revenge?"

"I never heard of that," I said loyally.

Celeste, Plumsie, Lenny, whichever one it was, was right, of course: We're taught to say that.

But it was the very first time I'd ever said it and known better. For when Deem was convicted of drug dealing, and then killed mysteriously during our Easter vacation, I'd believed the rumors that the drug lords had copied descriptions of The Sevens Revenge to take suspicion off themselves.

Thanks to the journal, I finally knew better.

Thanks to the journal, I knew better, I knew more, I

knew then that in a world so full of cunning and concealment, I needed all the help I could get . . . whether I owned a restaurant, had a chain of them, or worked as a chef in one.

No matter what I did, or where I did it. I'd best get my butt back to the books, to The Hill, to The Sevens.

16

Before I left, Annette Plummer showed me Celeste's room, exactly as it had always been, still waiting for her . . . across the hall from a smaller room where Star lived.

I asked her if she wanted me to put the suitcase in Fen's room, and she answered that she'd like that.

That was when I slipped the journal into my pocket. I must have always known I would not leave it for Fen to read, for I had never mentioned it.

Lark took me back down in the elevator.

"Did you talk a lot about Mr. Nels?" he asked me.

"Enough to make me suspicious," I said.

He laughed as though I'd said something funny. He said "That Mr. Tobias? He's full of suspicions. At one time he even suspected Miss Annette. And he's always snooping around in the Captain's life. He could be right about the Captain."

"Why do you say that?"

"The Captain's a man who likes what money can buy. A man who drives an Avanti around likes what money can buy. Her money bought it, of course. And the boat. Imagine wanting a boat when you work on one? But it's quite a boat, and she bought it."

"What were Nels and she like together?"

"When he was small she called him Little King Tut, and he was, too. The master spoiled him rotten. Remember, it wasn't her brother. Not a blood relative at all. . . . She was always jealous of Mr. Nels. He came along so unexpectedly, and he was a real Plummer—and a male in the bargain. The master focused all his attention on the boy, see, because the Mrs. passed away. But Mr. Nels adored Miss Annette. He tried his best to please her, always. Poor Mr. Nels."

"And how did he feel about Celeste?"

"She's an itch with a b in front of it, Mr. Fell."

I laughed and so did he.

Then I said, "What do you really think happened to him, Lark?"

"Someone murdered him, Mr. Fell. . . . That school friend of his, maybe . . . or someone closer." He looked around him in the small elevator, as though the culprit could be riding down with us. "Someone very close, maybe."

When we hit the first floor, he hung on to me. Someone should have been taking *him* up and down in the elevator, not the other way around.

He said, "That day Jack Kennedy was shot is like a bad dream. It wasn't real and yet it was. And I don't think we'll ever know the whole truth about that or this."

The next day before I checked in at Le Rêve, I tore a few pages out of the journal: the ones that described how Lenny and Nels named their trees Celeste, winning admission to Sevens…and at the very end, the pages about Lenny Last going to Cottersville to perform The Sevens Revenge on Deem.

Both Lenny Last and Deem were dead. The score was even.

I made some phone calls next and found out the address of George Tobias. Then I wrapped the journal up and mailed it to him.

It was his case, after all; he should be the one to solve it.

As for any immediate punishment due the Captain, I was betting on Celeste.

I was betting that with Celeste back aboard the *Seastar*, *The Ancient Mariner* would read like the story of Little Bo Peep.

17

That September I returned to Gardner and to Sevens House.

Not everyone on The Hill had resigned himself to the fact we were now a coed institution.

There were pickets out with signs reading BETTER DEAD THAN COED, and WOE, MEN! WOMEN!

There was only one new member of Sevens, a junior named Parson Stalker.

He told The Sevens he was assigned to that he had named his tree Dazzler, after his horse.

He moved in right across the hall from me.

I'd walked over to introduce myself and tell him whatever he might want to know about life on campus as a Sevens.

He was sitting in a leather chair with his back to the door. He was smoking. The view in front of him was of The Tower, where the Sevens had sung him into the club . . . and where we ate evenings, separate from and better than the others at Gardner School.

"Hello there!" I called out to him. "If you have permission to smoke, do it down in the smoker, first floor."

There was no response. He didn't move a muscle.

He was reading a book by James Tiptree, Jr.

"I'm John Fell from across the hall!" I said.

He actually blew a few smoke rings, reminding me of Annette Plummer that Sunday morning I'd gone to see her.

The book he was holding up was called *Her Smoke Rose Up Forever.* His did too; maybe he couldn't see me through it. I went closer until I was right in front of him and then finally he looked up at me and said, "Who're you?"

"Fell!" I said. "No smoking!" I was teed off.

Then I saw the cord coming down behind his ear and inside his shirt collar.

He put his fingers to his lips making a shhh gesture. He pointed to his cigarette.

I shook my head. "No way. Put it out!"

He laughed and gave me a beseeching look as though he was saying "Please?"

"Stalker, butt it!"

"Parson," he said. "Parr. Who're you?"

I told him again.

He was a turn-head, kind of good-looking; male or female, you'd want to be sure you were seeing right.

He belonged in movies, on the slick pages of magazines, and up on billboards. He had dark eyes and black hair and he was tanned. White, perfect teeth. A mole just to the left of a dimple. Forget Tom Cruise!

He put out his cigarette, shrugging. "Okay," he said. Then he pointed to the hearing aid and said, "I'm deaf. This alerts you more than it helps me hear. I read lips."

"You speak good."

"I do everything good." He laughed.

"Yeah, you even brag good."

He laughed again and nodded. "I brag good."

"Welcome to Sevens." I grinned at him.

He said, "You're all lucky to have me," and he grinned back.

▣

He said what?

I was late for Science. I was up to explain Lamarckism that morning, so my mind was on acquired characteristics . . . but he said *what*?

I told myself probably Stalker was just a wiseacre, but you know the feeling you have when something says what you see is what you're getting?

There was that feeling.

There was that feeling, there was my forthcoming discussion of the French naturalist Jean Baptiste de Lamarck, and there was a September rain that added whole new dimensions to the meaning of the word wet.

I was running through it when I saw her.

And she is somebody I am always seeing, even though it is never her. She is at bus stops as I go by in a car, in crowds I see from buses, at the backs of restaurants until I get closer, and again and again flying with me in dreams.

But that September day in the pouring rain I swore that I saw Delia on that campus.

By the time classes were finished, the rain was too.

The late-afternoon sun brought my sanity back, I believed, and the beginnings of autumn colored the campus.

In my mailbox was a letter from George Tobias and one from Keats.

Keats' first.

Yes, I'm in love and that's why you haven't heard from me! My life would be perfect if it were not for her. She calls me Bleeps, because she says what she wants to call me would be bleeped out. And DON'T tell me it's really Fen, because it really isn't. Maybe she isn't real, but she is a force, Fell! I was almost glad to get back to school to be away from her! Fen is coming this weekend, without her. Can't wait. He's my fella, Fell.

xxxxx Keats

P.S. He doesn't know anything about the journal and I'd just as soon keep it that way now that I've met Celeste. I don't want Fen swallowing that mystique of hers. It's bad enough without written confirmation of her power! . . . Do you really think Tobias will take it to the police?

Tobias' letter answered her question. He had already called me in August, to thank me for sending the journal.

Dear Fell,

A detective who investigated the case years ago is having a look at the diary, comparing it with the Captain's testimony.

It'll take time, but I think we're onto something. Keep quiet about it.

The detective knew your dad. He also wants to know about your mother. Seems he dated her before your dad did. His name is Tom Bernagozzi. Would your mother mind if he called her? I'll keep in touch. Thanks!

G.T.

I was in a good mood, glad to be back.

I went up to my room in Sevens House to drop off my raincoat and give Mom a buzz.

At the end of our conversation I told her that the detective working on the Nels Plummer case had known Dad.

"What's his name?" she said.

"Tom Bernagozzi," I said.

"You've got to be kidding!" she said.

"I'm not," I said.

"Tommy!" she said. "I didn't know he was still around."

I said, "Well, he is, and he's asking for you. I'm supposed to find out if he can call you."

"If he can *call* me?" She laughed. "He can do more

than *call* me. Him with *his* eyes?"

"Yeah, but what about Mr. Lopez?" I said.

"What about him?" she said. "He's just a neighbor."

I changed into shorts and Keds. I felt like running. At least that kind of running had a purpose.

I was ready to go when I smelled cigarette smoke again. I heard the sound of female laughter.

Parson Stalker was breaking two rules at once this time: smoking above first floor, and entertaining a female in his room on a weekday.

I thought right: Woe Men, Women!

I went across to speak to them, to get her out of there . . . fast.

She was sitting on the windowsill facing Stalker, wearing something red, smoking a cigarette.

When she saw me, she stood up.

She looked at me, the same way she had always looked at me . . . her eyes all over my face, the pitch-black hair spilling down her back.

I felt my knees almost give and my insides flip.

I said, "Delia?"

"No, her sister," she said. "April." She was coming toward me with her hand out. "April Tremble," she said. "And you must be Fell."